Orange Thyme
Bay Cozy Myst___ ____ ____ _

By Leena Clover

Chapter 1

Anna Butler filled a piping bag with cream cheese frosting and started working on her orange thyme cupcakes. Her book café was set for a grand opening in three days and she was making some last minute tweaks to her signature recipe. Anna had run Bayside Books, the popular Dolphin Bay bookstore for twenty years. Now she had leased the space next door, knocked down the wall between the two stores and created a cozy space where people could enjoy a hot or cold drink along with her gourmet cupcakes.

Anna had come a long way in the past two years. Her husband John had been taken suddenly, leaving her a widow at 55. Just when she was coming to terms with her grief, she was diagnosed with the dreaded C, breast cancer. Anna battled the disease bravely, going through the long and tedious treatments with a brave face. Now she was ready to get back in her groove and start her own café, a dream she had cherished for a while.

Anna swirled the frosting over a freshly baked cupcake and placed it before the young woman sitting at the kitchen table.

Cassie Butler, Anna's 36 year old daughter, looked up with a frown.

"I just finished breakfast, Mom," she muttered. "And I can't taste any more cupcakes. My pants are beginning to split at the seams."

"Stop exaggerating," Anna said lightly. "I need to get these right for opening night."

Cassie picked up the cupcake, took a small bite and moaned with pleasure.

"These are yum! You have nothing to worry about."

"You think the people of Dolphin Bay will go for these?" Anna asked.

"They are going to line up outside your door, just to get a whiff of these," Cassie nodded loyally.

Cassie Butler was currently at a loose end. She had left her home at 16, lured by the bright lights of Hollywood. She won an Oscar award at 21 and basked in its glory for a while. Her life had been a roller coaster ride in the years since then, with two failed marriages, a declining career and a surprise comeback via a Mexican telenovela. She had been living in the lap of fame and luxury when her business manager absconded with most of her fortune, leaving her high and dry with a big tax bill. Cassie had come home to lick her wounds and look after her ailing mother.

"Did you lock up the store properly last night?" Anna asked Cassie.

Cassie could be a bit absent minded.

"Don't you trust me, Mom?" Cassie asked with a pout. "I'm actually old enough to follow simple instructions."

"No need to get your panties in a wad, missy. You forget to do a lot of things."

Cassie sulked for a while. Anna ignored her and decided to add more orange zest to her frosting. She wanted the citrus flavor to really pop.

"We never talked about the wine festival at Mystic Hill," Cassie said after a while. "Did you enjoy yourself?"

Anna's cheeks turned red.

"It was nice. I didn't expect so many people would turn up."

"You thought you would have Gino to yourself, huh?" Cassie teased.

"Don't be silly. Why would I think that? I knew it was an open event."

"But you were a special guest, weren't you?"

"Gino did make me feel special," Anna agreed. "He introduced me to so many people I barely remember their names."

Gino Mancini was a well known figure in Dolphin Bay. He owned the famous Mystic Hill winery and the vineyards that produced the excellent local wine. He had been a decorated veteran, a city detective and police chief of the Dolphin Bay police force. He had retired from the force a few years ago and devoted himself to the family business. Cassie thought he had a tendre for Anna. Anna's friends agreed.

"Did you have a good time though?" Cassie asked.

"I did," Anna nodded. "And I drank way too much wine."

"When is Gino taking you out on a proper date?"

Anna blushed a bit more.

"Tell me about the concert," she said, evading Cassie's question. "Did you have a good time last night?"

"The best!" Cassie said, nodding eagerly. "You missed it, Mom. That girl was so good."

"I don't like this new fangled music, Cassie. I don't understand it."

"But that's just it," Cassie argued. "She sang the blues. What could be more old fashioned than that? Her voice is pure gold. They are calling her a young Ella."

"After Ella Fitzgerald?" Anna asked doubtfully. "That's high praise indeed."

"I think she's worth it."

Anna was glad to find Cassie had enjoyed herself. There wasn't much for her to do in Dolphin Bay. She was almost like an outsider, having been away for twenty years. Cassie spent her days lying around the pool, watching movies or talking to her fitness trainer friend Bobby on the phone. Bobby lived in Los Angeles and was always too busy to pay a visit.

The local resort was hosting a young singer and one of

Cassie's high school buddies had invited her to go along. Anna had literally forced her to go.

"How was Teddy's wife?" Anna asked.

"She's cool," Cassie said with a shrug. "She's watched all my movies. They have a Cassandra Butler movie night every month!"

"Don't sound so surprised," Anna smiled. "I bet you still have thousands of fans around the country."

"I don't know, Mom. I think I'm history."

"You just need a new release," Anna consoled. "You'll be back at the top before you know it."

"Enough already, Mom." Cassie flared suddenly. "I don't need that kind of pressure."

"Take as long as you like. I can really use your help at the café, Cassie. But keeping you here would be selfish of me. You are meant for greater things."

Cassie looked mutinous.

"Aren't you getting late, Mom?"

Anna started loading the dishwasher with all her baking utensils.

"Those petitions worked like a charm, didn't they?" she mused.

"You have plenty of friends in Dolphin Bay, Mom. No

matter what Lara Crawford says."

Anna's face hardened a bit.

Lara Crawford was the town mayor and Anna's nemesis. She had made it her personal mission to make life difficult for Anna. According to Lara, Anna was guilty of murdering her husband John. Lara went around bad mouthing Anna at every opportunity. But she didn't stop there. She had pulled some strings to make sure Anna didn't get the license for her café. Then she had gone and reopened the investigation into John's death.

Anna's friends had canvassed the locals and collected signatures declaring support for the proposed café. The powers that be had finally caved in and given her the green light to open her café. But Anna was still on the hook for being involved in her husband's death.

"John and I were together for thirty five years," Anna said, blinking back a tear. "We had our ups and downs but we loved each other unconditionally. I would never do anything to harm him."

"I know, Mom," Cassie said loyally. "I believe you."

"What about those classes you were going to enroll in?" Anna asked, steering the conversation to a neutral topic.

"They seem a bit expensive. I can learn it online for free."

"Why don't I sign you up? My treat."

"That's not necessary," Cassie hedged. "I am not even sure I'm cut out for cooking. I might be better off learning film production or something."

"I think you should work on your GED first."

Cassie pretended she didn't hear her mother.

"Aren't you meeting the Firecrackers today?" she asked, referring to Anna's special friends.

"Mary and Julie are meeting me at the store," Anna said, perking up. "We are going to give the café a thorough cleaning before we arrange all the furniture."

"Again?" Cassie scoffed. "How many times have you done that already?"

"I want to get it right, Cassie. I want the space to feel cozy and welcoming."

"The fireplace makes it cozy alright," Cassie assured her. "And all that overstuffed furniture you have collected seems perfect for the place."

"I hope so," Anna said enthusiastically. "We are going to string some lights on the outside along with the big banner Julie ordered."

"What about the chalkboard? Is it here yet?"

Mother and daughter chatted about all the chores they had to get done before the café opened to the public. Anna knew Cassie had planned a surprise party for her the day before the opening. A select group of her friends had been invited. It was going to be held at the café on the evening before the inauguration. Anna was secretly looking forward to it.

"Have you looked at the time?" Anna exclaimed suddenly. "Time for me to go, kiddo."

Anna checked her face in the hall mirror, waved goodbye to Cassie and hurried out. She was cycling to her bookstore a few minutes later, a faint smile of anticipation on her face.

Life was looking up for Anna Butler.

Chapter 2

Cassie lingered over her coffee. She had enjoyed herself at the concert the previous night. Teddy Fowler's wife had gushed all over her, making her feel important. She now had an open invitation to Sunday dinner at the Fowler residence.

Cassie placed a call to her friend Bobby. Bobby appeared on the screen a moment later, dripping with sweat.

"I'm doing lunges," he announced. "Can I call you back, sweetie?"

Cassie hung up and looked around her. She cleared the breakfast things and wiped down the counters half heartedly. The turquoise pool beckoned. She went to her room to change into her bikini. Cassie swam her usual twenty laps in the pool and settled down on her favorite cabana. She had a stack of magazines beside her in case she got bored along with her phone which hardly ever rang nowadays. The only people who called her were Bobby or her mother.

Cassie was just about to doze off with her arms behind her head when the phone rang. It was an unknown number. Cassie ignored it but the phone continued to ring persistently. She finally sat up on her elbows and answered the phone desultorily.

"Hello?"

"Cassie! What took you so long?"

"Mom!" Cassie sighed. "I'm out by the pool."

"Listen to me carefully, Cassie."

Cassie picked up the urgency in Anna's voice.

"I'm at the police station."

"What?"

Cassie sat up with a jerk, flinging her feet down on the floor.

"What are you doing there, Mom? Is everything alright?"

"Calm down and listen carefully. I found a dead body in the store when I went in this morning. I called the cops, of course. Now they have brought me in for questioning."

Cassie found it difficult to breathe.

"What do you mean, dead body?" she parroted. "Like an actual dead person?"

Anna became impatient.

"That's what I said, girl. Get Julie or Mary and come here."

The call ended abruptly.

Cassie's legs wobbled as she stood up and began pacing around the pool. She dialed Julie, her mother's friend.

Julie Walsh was a romance author of some repute. She was always busy writing her next book.

"Hey Cassie? Can I call you back? I'm in the middle of …"

"Listen up, Aunt Julie!" Cassie broke in. "Mom's at the police station. They found a dead body at the bookstore."

Julie took charge.

"Get dressed. I'm coming right over."

Cassie was standing outside the white picket fence when Julie drove up in her big SUV. She barely stopped long enough for Cassie to get in.

"Mary's visiting her kid in San Jose," she said grimly. "So it's just you and me for now."

Cassie asked for Teddy Fowler as soon as they entered the police station. Teddy must have heard her. He peeped out of a small room and beckoned them over.

"Where is she?" Julie demanded. "Where are you holding her?"

"Is my mom under arrest?" Cassie spoke up. "I want to see her."

"Calm down, ladies," Teddy said smoothly. "We did bring Anna Butler in for questioning. It's just routine at this time."

"She didn't do anything!" Cassie said fiercely.

"That remains to be determined," Teddy shrugged. "As of now, she is just the person who discovered the body. But we can't overlook the fact that the dead guy was found on her property."

"So what?" Julie thundered. "That doesn't make her a suspect."

"She's the only one who had access to the shop," Teddy pointed out. "We will sort all that out when we question her. Why don't I get you ladies some coffee?"

"Can I talk to her?" Cassie asked again.

"She'll be out soon," Teddy promised. "You can take her home then."

"I think we are in for a long wait," Julie sighed. "I'll take that coffee now, Detective."

Cassie fired off a few text messages to Bobby. He called her back immediately. Cassie spoke to him in a hushed voice, oblivious to the glares a desk clerk shot at her.

Teddy ushered Anna out half an hour later. She fell into Julie's arms without a word.

"Let's go home," she said before Cassie could ask her anything.

Cassie put the coffee on when they arrived at the Butler residence. Julie pulled out a bottle of whiskey from a kitchen cabinet and poured some into Anna's cup, ignoring her protests.

"You need some liquid courage today, Anna. Drink up and start at the beginning."

Mary hurried in through the kitchen door, looking flustered.

"I just got back from San Jose."

She pulled Anna into a tight hug.

"Are you okay, sweetie? What happened?"

"We are all waiting to hear that," Cassie said pointedly.

"I went to the store this morning, just like every day," Anna began. "Mrs. Chang was coming out of Paradise Market. She waved at me and I waved back."

"Go on …" Cassie was impatient.

"I stood under the magnolia tree," Anna continued. "Something felt a bit odd. I couldn't really figure out what. The sidewalk was covered in a blanket of blossoms and the air was full of their heady scent."

Cassie tapped her foot on the floor, wishing her mother would hurry up.

"Tell us what you found," Julie said, gently prodding Anna to get to the point.

"This part is important," Anna insisted. "I could tell something was out of place. I took my key out of my bag and started putting it in the lock. That's when I realized the door was open."

Julie, Mary and Cassie all exclaimed together.

"What did you do?" Mary asked in a whisper.

"Tell me you called the police right away?" Julie roared.

Anna shook her head.

"I looked around. Everything appeared fine. So I went in."

"That was a stupid move," Julie told her. "What if an intruder had been lying in wait for you inside?"

"It was 9 AM in the morning on a bright summer day," Anna said lightly. "I had nothing to be afraid of."

"Tell us what happened next, Mom," Cassie said impatiently. "Had the store been robbed?"

"Everything looked just fine," Anna said. "I heaved a sigh of relief. Who's going to steal a bunch of books? And most of our purchases are by card so there isn't much cash lying around."

"So you went in," Julie prompted.

"I walked over to the new section," Anna explained, referring to the extension where the café was going to be. "That's when I found a foot sticking out. I called the police right away."

"I would have screamed the place down," Mary said.

"Did you take a look at the body?" Julie asked curiously. "Anyone we know?"

"He looked like a handyman John had hired once to fix the roof. But I can't be sure."

"What was he doing in the store?" Cassie asked.

She was beginning to wonder if she had forgotten to lock the door the previous night. She had been in a hurry to get to the concert. She remembered tidying up the store and she remembered walking out. But had she pulled the door shut behind her? Anna hadn't said anything about it yet.

"Who knows?" Anna shrugged.

"This doesn't look good for you, Anna," Julie said. "You wanna bet Lara Crawford is going to raise a big stink about this?"

Cassie's frown deepened as she connected the dots.

"Aunt Julie's right, Mom. Now you are wanted for two murders."

"Hush, Cassie," Mary said. "Your mother is innocent."

"I know that, Aunt Mary, and you know that," Cassie muttered. "But that won't stop the police from making her life hell."

Anna's face had turned green. Julie rubbed her back and shot a warning look at Cassie.

"This is not one of your thriller films, Cassie," Julie warned. "Stop exaggerating."

Mary wove her arm through Anna's and Julie did the same.

"We are here for you, Anna," Julie said. "You don't need to worry about a thing."

Cassie looked at the three friends and felt a warm glow inside. The Firecrackers as they called themselves had been through a lot together. She was sure they would stand by her mother through this latest storm in her life.

"What about the bookstore?" she asked her mother. "I guess we can't go back there today?"

"The police have sealed the store," Anna sighed. "We have to wait until they give us the all-clear."

"What about the café, Anna?" Julie asked. "Our grand opening is two days away."

Cassie saw Anna's shoulders slump. They had all worked really hard to ensure the café opening was a success. Invitations had gone out and advertisements had been placed in the local papers of the neighboring towns. A large crowd had been expected.

"It's a blessing in disguise, Mom," she said, plastering a wide smile on her face. "Now you have more time to tweak your orange thyme cupcake recipe."

Chapter 3

The bright summer sunshine wasn't doing much for Cassie's mood the next morning. She stifled a yawn and stirred her coffee moodily, letting it grow cold. Anna was making mushroom and cheddar omelets for breakfast. Cassie watched as her mother flipped the golden omelets and plated them. Anna placed a stack of toast on the table along with a crock of fresh churned butter from the local Daisy Hollow farm.

"Who's the third plate for?" Cassie asked, not feeling up to entertaining a guest that early in the morning.

"It's for Meg. I invited her for breakfast."

Cassie let out a rude exclamation.

"What do you have against her?" Anna asked. "You should be thanking the lord she has found us."

"Why are you so infatuated with her, Mom?"

"She is my granddaughter. I am not just infatuated with her. I love her."

"You barely know her."

"And whose fault is that?" Anna muttered under her breath.

She climbed up on a stool and looked at Cassie pleadingly.

"I don't blame you for what happened twenty years ago, sweetie. You were in a bad place and you did what you thought was best for you."

"You didn't think so then!" Cassie said darkly.

"No, I didn't," Anna sighed. "Neither did your father. We wanted to raise that child as our own. She should have grown up right here in this house, where she belonged."

"Do you know how small this town is?" Cassie asked. "I would have been a laughing stock."

"We could have spun it any way," Anna shrugged. "But there's no use talking about all that now. What's done is done."

Cassie stared moodily in the distance. Glimpses of her past flashed before her eyes. She had thought her life was over when she got pregnant at sixteen. All her dreams of being a famous Hollywood star had shattered right then. There was no way she was going to get her big break as a teen mom. So she had chosen to give the child up for adoption. Her parents had been against the idea. They wanted to raise the baby as their own. They were young and healthy and had the means to give the child a good life. But Cassie had been adamant.

"You are so fortunate, Cassie," Anna said softly. "Life is giving you another chance. Embrace it with an open heart."

"What do we really know about her, huh?" Cassie argued. "How can you be sure she is telling the truth? She could be an impostor."

"Really, Cassie?" Anna shook her head sadly. "You don't believe that."

"I'm serious, Mom. We need to confirm her identity. Get a DNA test or something."

"You watch too many movies, girl," Anna spat. "I don't need any test to tell me who she is. I can feel it here, in my heart."

"Whatever!" Cassie rolled her eyes and stabbed her omelet with a fork. She began eating mindlessly, shoveling anything she could lay her hands on into her mouth.

"Meg will be here any minute," Anna said, placing a plate in the oven to keep it warm. "You be nice to her. Or make yourself scarce."

Truth be told, Cassie was curious about Meg. She had been shocked to the core when Meg revealed who she was. How was she supposed to guess that the young girl she had met around town and casually offered a job was the child she had given up for adoption twenty years ago?

Where had she been all these years? What had her life been like? Cassie supposed she should feel some kind of warmth toward this person who was her own flesh and blood. Maybe she just wasn't cut out to be a mother. Giving Meg up might have been the best thing she did for her.

"I'm going for a swim. You can have your precious Meg to yourself, Mom."

"Stay here for a while and say hello. It costs nothing to be polite."

Cassie topped up her coffee and stood up to get some cream from the refrigerator. She liked her coffee to be really milky and sweet.

"Why don't you get the paper from the porch?" Anna asked. "I forgot to bring it in this morning."

Cassie made a big show of going to the front door and picking up the paper. She handed it to Anna with a bow. Two minutes later, Anna let out a small cry as she stared at the front page.

"What is it, Mom?" Cassie asked, trying to read the newspaper over her mother's shoulder.

Anna's face was splashed over the front page of the Dolphin Bay Chronicle.

"Husband Killer Strikes Again", ran the bold print.

The story explained how Anna Butler, a local resident who was the top suspect in her husband's suspicious death was now implicated in another murder.

Cassie took one look at Anna's face and snatched the paper away from her.

"Don't read that trash."

"The Chronicle is not trash," Anna protested. "We have relied on it to give us the local news all our lives."

"They seem to have crossed over into tabloid territory now."

"This is going to be bad for business," Anna frowned. "People might boycott the café if they believe all this nonsense."

"You want my advice?" Cassie asked. "Distance yourself from all this. In fact, why don't we go somewhere for a couple of weeks? Bobby will gladly put us up."

"I'm not running away," Anna said firmly. "That will only make me look guilty."

"Don't tell me you want to go sleuthing again, Mom. I really think you should stay out of it this time and let the police do their job."

"You want me to trust your pal Teddy?" Anna cried. "He thinks I am guilty."

Cassie hesitated.

"He didn't exactly say that."

"I'm not going to sit around and wait for him to slap the cuffs on my wrists."

Cassie took one look at Anna's mulish expression and knew she was fighting a losing battle.

"I can see that," she sighed. "So what's the plan?"

"I don't know yet," Anna said, "but I need to defend myself. Julie and Mary will agree with me."

Cassie sat down and took Anna's hand in hers.

"I'll help too, Mom."

Her lips stretched into a smile as her eyes twinkled with mischief.

"Don't forget Gino. I'm sure he'll do what he can to help you through this."

Anna blushed.

"Now you're being silly."

The doorbell rang and Cassie went over to open the door. Meg stood outside, clutching a bunch of wildflowers in her hand. Cassie noticed the threadbare tee she was wearing and decided it came from a superstore rather than an upscale mall.

Meg gave her a wide grin and motioned toward the flowers.

"These are for Anna."

"Come in and give them to her yourself," Cassie said, opening the door wide.

She wondered if she should hug Meg. She got her answer when Meg breezed in and walked straight into the kitchen. Anna opened her arms wide and hugged the skinny girl.

"Your bones are sticking out," Anna grumbled goodnaturedly. "We'll have to do something about that."

"I eat a lot," Meg said with a shrug. "I'm just blessed with a fast metabolism."

"Wait till you're 30," Cassie said. "The pounds will start piling up before you know it."

Anna fussed over Meg while she tucked into her omelet.

"What do you like to eat?" Anna asked. "I generally make avocado toast for breakfast but I thought you might prefer eggs."

"I love avocadoes!" Meg exclaimed brightly. "That's one thing about California I really like. Plenty of avocadoes and oranges."

"I almost forgot. I made orange juice!" Anna exclaimed, rushing toward the refrigerator.

She pulled out a carafe of freshly squeezed juice and poured some in a glass.

"I have an orange tree in my backyard," Cassie said. "Doesn't get fresher than that."

"Is that in Los Angeles?" Meg asked eagerly. "Can we go there sometime?"

Cassie's face fell.

"I guess so. The house is listed on the market. It will be sold soon."

"We can still go and stay in a hotel," Anna stepped in. "Cassie can show us the sights."

The back door flung open and Julie rushed in, followed by Mary.

"Don't read the Chronicle," she began and stopped mid-sentence when she spotted the newspaper on the table.

"I've already seen it," Anna said grimly. "And I'm not giving up without a fight."

"That's my girl!" Julie said, thumping Anna on the back.

"Have you heard?" Mary asked. "The Annual Rose Show is going ahead as planned."

"But I thought they canceled due to lack of funds?" Anna asked.

"A big donation came in at the last minute," Mary said. "The Garden Club met this morning and finalized the date. The Annual Rose Show will be held in the second week of August like every year."

"What about the venue?" Julie asked. "Are they still fighting over it?"

"We took a vote on that," Mary told them.

She had been a member of the local Garden Club since she got married. She was the secretary for the current year.

"Where is this show?" Cassie asked, feigning interest.

"It's at the Botanical Gardens," Mary explained. "It will be a two day event. We believe it will be a big draw for tourists."

"Who's heading the Rose Show committee?" Julie asked. "Not that sour puss Agnes?"

Mary grimaced.

"Nothing I could do about it. She's the finest rose grower in Dolphin Bay."

"You know what that means?" Julie asked, her hands on her hips. "She'll never let Anna in."

Chapter 4

Anna brewed her first cup of coffee the next morning and decided to bake some cupcakes. She didn't like to sit still. Now that the bookstore was out of limits for her, she found she had a lot of time on her hands.

Cassie came out of her room, dressed in fancy exercise clothes. They came from a website with a funny name. Was it orange or lime, Anna tried to remember. It was definitely some kind of citrus fruit.

"I'm going for a run, Mom."

Cassie waved at her and stepped out. Anna settled down to enjoy some peace and quiet with her coffee. She must have dozed off a bit. The next thing she knew, Cassie was back in the kitchen, slamming the refrigerator door as she grabbed some cream for her coffee.

"Did you sleep well, Mom?" Cassie asked her.

"Very well, thank you." Anna was defensive.

She knew what was coming next.

"You are taking your meds, right?" Cassie asked. "They are an important part of your recovery."

"Of course I am taking them," Anna said sharply.

"What about your vitamins?" Cassie said. "You should really add turmeric shots to your diet. Bobby says …"

"I don't have to do everything Bobby says."

"Bobby knows all the latest trends," Cassie pressed. "He charges thousands of dollars for this kind of advice. And we are getting it for free."

Anna thought Cassie was a bit too influenced by Bobby. She had never met this paragon of health who looked like a Greek God but she already hated him.

"What do you want for breakfast?"

"Seriously, Mom. You should add golden milk to the café menu."

"Green smoothies, turmeric milk, chia pudding – I don't think anyone has heard of these fads in Dolphin Bay, Cassie. I want to offer comfort food that people will come back for. Hearty sandwiches and soups, cupcakes, pies and really good coffee."

Cassie looked disappointed. Anna relented.

"We need to finalize our menu anyway. Why don't we add one of your items? But strictly on a trial basis and only on the chalkboard menu."

"You won't be sorry, Mom."

Anna realized Cassie had been peeling bananas while she talked to her. She watched her add them to the blender along with some fresh berries and mangoes and a handful of baby spinach.

"I'm not having any of that, Cassie."

Mother and daughter argued for a while. Anna finally agreed to drink a bit of the smoothie before eating her toast. The doorbell chimed before she could admit the green stuff was actually quite tasty.

"Is Meg coming over again?" Cassie asked as she went out to open the door.

Anna was surprised to see Cassie come back with Gino Mancini trailing behind her. Frantically, she tried to remember if she was still in her pajamas.

"Good Morning, Anna," Gino greeted her with a smile. "You look beautiful this morning."

"Err…thanks," Anna mumbled.

"Have you had breakfast?" Cassie asked him. "How about a tropical smoothie? I just made Mom try one."

"I don't mind," Gino told her. "I'm a smoothie man myself. But it's hard to get one in our little town."

"See?" Cassie trained her eyes on Anna. "You need to sell these at the café."

"Never mind all that, Cassie," Anna said.

"You must be wondering what I am doing here so early in the morning," Gino began, sensing that Anna was looking worried. "I am afraid the news is not good."

"Don't keep anything from me, Gino," Anna said, squaring her shoulders. "I can handle it."

Gino took a sip of the smoothie Cassie poured for him and gave her a thumbs up.

"I heard from my sources at the police station. They confirmed that you are now a suspect in this latest investigation. I am not sure why but I am trying to find out."

"That's ridiculous!" Cassie exclaimed. "What's Mom got to do with some random guy who dropped dead in our bookstore?"

"He didn't just die, Cassie," Gino sighed. "We don't have an autopsy report yet but it looks like he was attacked. Word on the street is Anna knew him well."

Anna took a deep breath as she tried to process Gino's news.

"Thanks for the heads up, Gino. I really appreciate it."

"I have my ear to the ground, Anna. I'll let you know as soon as I learn anything more."

"Please don't trouble yourself on my account."

"You don't have to be so formal, Anna. We are friends, aren't we? Friends look out for each other." Gino cleared his throat. "I know you will start snooping around. Just be careful, okay? And let me know if I can help in any way."

"I know why the police are after Mom," Cassie spoke up.

"I met Teddy Fowler on the Coastal Walk when I went for my run. He says the mayor tipped them off."

"So Lara Crawford strikes again," Anna said, slamming a fist on the counter. "Why am I not surprised?"

"Why is she pointing the finger at Anna?" Gino asked.

"Let's go into the living room and sit down," Anna suggested before Cassie could answer.

They had all been standing around the kitchen counter and Anna's feet were beginning to ache.

"Go on, Cassie," she said after they had all picked a seat.

"This Lara woman is like a broken record," Cassie said. "She says the dead guy was a contractor or handyman who did small jobs for people. He was working here when Dad died. He must have seen something. Mom knew that and she wanted to silence him."

"That's a big leap even for Lara," Anna said. "I don't even remember when that man worked here."

"Say he did work here on that fateful day," Gino mused. "Why would Anna wait until now to kill him?"

"It's because the police have reopened the old case," Cassie explained. "At least that's what Teddy told me Lara said."

"This is all pure speculation," Gino said. "Normally, this kind of stuff wouldn't fly but it has a certain weight coming from Lara. Unfortunately, her word means a lot in this town."

"So she will continue to harass Mom just because she can do it?" Cassie asked, outraged. "What did you ever do to her, Mom?"

"I have no idea," Anna said. "Your father and Lara were always good friends. They met for lunch once a month. I didn't have a problem with that. Lara came here for Thanksgiving or Christmas dinners. She was always polite to me. But she changed her tune after your father died, Cassie. Maybe she really believes I had something to do with John's death."

"I haven't known you that long," Gino said, "and I believe you are innocent. So what makes Lara doubt you?"

"I think she's just being petty and vindictive," Cassie spat.

"Maybe she knows something we don't," Gino said.

"Why doesn't she come forward and say it?" Anna asked. "I am not trying to hide anything. I'm ready to answer any questions she has."

"Lara Crawford is not going anywhere, Anna. I think you should forget about her and focus on this latest investigation. The police must be getting ready to question you soon."

"I don't have much to tell them, Gino. I barely knew that man."

Cassie addressed Gino. "Can you anticipate what they might ask her?"

"The usual questions," Gino shrugged. He made sure Anna

was paying attention. "Where were you that evening at a certain time? Can anyone vouch for you? How many people had access to the store?"

Anna grew tense.

"I was home that night, alone. I had a headache, remember?"

Gino had invited Anna to dinner at the winery. She was looking forward to it but had to beg off at the last minute because she wasn't feeling well. Now she wished she had just popped some aspirin and spent the evening with Gino.

"I had thought of coming over with my pot roast but I didn't want to disturb you," Gino clucked, reading Anna's mind. "Hindsight's always twenty-twenty, isn't it?"

"It's not your fault," Anna assured him. "Who knew I would need an alibi for that night?"

"Wasn't Cassie home too?" Gino asked.

"Cassie was at a concert. Julie and Mary were both busy with something. So it was just me."

"Just tell them the truth, Anna," Gino said softly. "Things will work out."

"I am going to make sure they do," Anna said grimly.

Gino had a meeting with his vineyard manager so he stood up to leave. Anna walked him to the door.

"Thank you for coming, Gino. I sleep easier knowing you

are on my side."

Chapter 5

Anna had a lot on her mind that evening as she put all her might into kneading the pasta dough. The day had started with Gino bringing unfavorable news. Anna had been so restless she hadn't done anything right all day. Her cupcakes had burned because she forgot to set the oven timer. The frosting she was trying out had split. Then she had sparred with Cassie for an hour over whether to ask Meg for dinner or not.

Finally, Anna had put her foot down. It was her house and she could invite anyone she wanted. Cassie could take it or leave it. Cassie had stomped out and settled into her favorite cabana by the pool. She had been out there in the sun for hours.

Anna decided that times were desperate and she needed to clear her head.

When Anna was stressed, she made pasta. There was something therapeutic about rolling and kneading the dough and stirring the homemade tomato sauce. Anna just hoped Meg liked ravioli. She had already made a big bowl of salad and a pan full of her special tiramisu.

There was a knock on the kitchen door and Anna wiped her hands on her apron before pulling it open. Dylan Woods stood outside with a brown paper package in his hands. His family owned the local Daisy Hollow farm. Anna enjoyed some special privileges with them as a preferred customer.

"Come in and have some coffee," Anna said, welcoming him with a hug.

"I gotta run, Anna," he said apologetically. "This is the ricotta you ordered. Made fresh today."

Anna almost asked him to stay for dinner and then remembered Meg was coming.

"What's he doing here?" Cassie grumbled as she came in through the French doors.

"Nice welcome, Princess!" Dylan drawled. "Got too much sun?"

Anna winced as she looked at Cassie's face and arms. She was definitely going to be in pain later.

"Don't mind her, Dylan. Cassie's in a bad mood."

"But I just got here," Dylan joked.

Cassie went to her room in a huff.

"Do you have some aloe vera?" Dylan asked seriously. "She's going to need it."

Anna thanked Dylan and saw him off. She went into the garden to pick some fresh basil and oregano. The chopped herbs went into the ricotta cheese. Anna had a pile of ravioli ready in no time.

The doorbell rang, announcing Meg's arrival. Anna rushed

out with a wide smile on her face. She was looking forward to this visit. There was a lot she wanted to ask Meg.

Meg sat at the kitchen counter, sipping the soda Anna had pressed in her hands.

"I hope you like ravioli," Anna said. "You are part Italian, you know."

"Really?" Meg asked, her eyes widening with interest.

"My parents were Italian," Anna explained. "My grandparents came to this country at the turn of the last century."

"I love pasta," Meg assured her. "Can I help you set the table?"

"You just sit back and relax," Anna beamed. "We are going to have a nice family dinner and get to know each other."

"Sounds great," Meg nodded.

Anna had pulled out the good china and set the table in the formal dining room. She lit the tapers and yelled at Cassie to come out.

"What's going on here, Mom?" Cassie asked cattily as she came out. "Why are you rolling out the red carpet?"

Anna saw Meg's eyes flicker and sensed her disappointment. She placed both hands firmly on the girl's bony shoulders.

"My only granddaughter has come to dinner, that's why."

Cassie mutely sat down opposite Meg and served herself a hefty portion of salad.

"How did you find us, Meg?" she asked, shoving a forkful of salad in her mouth. "I opted for a closed adoption all those years ago so my contact details were supposed to be private."

"Never mind all that," Anna said quickly. "I want to know about your life, Meg. Where did you grow up? Did you go to a good family?"

"It's a long story," Meg said hesitantly. "I don't remember a lot of it."

"What do you mean by that?" Cassie asked, cutting into her ravioli.

"Hush, Cassie. Let her speak." Anna looked at Meg encouragingly. "You can take as long as you like. I want to know everything."

"I pieced a lot of this together from my file," Meg began. "I was adopted by a family as a baby. I think I lived with them for about six years. I vaguely remember a brown haired woman and a young boy. He was my older brother."

"Did they give you up after six years?" Anna asked, mystified. "I didn't know people could do that."

"No," Meg sighed. "They died in a car accident. One of the relatives took the boy but none of them wanted me. So I went into the system."

"What system?" Cassie asked, her mouth full of cheese.

"The foster system," Anna said with a pang.

"She's right," Meg nodded. "I was placed with a foster family."

"Did they adopt you after some time?" Anna asked eagerly.

She had been a foster parent herself for several years and had a general idea of how the system worked. She and her husband John had never adopted anyone. Instead, they had chosen to take care of as many troubled kids as they could."

"No, they didn't," Meg said drily. "I was sent to a second foster family after a few days. Some weeks later, I was placed with a third foster family."

Anna swallowed a lump, sensing Meg had more to say.

"I was placed with 19 different foster families until I was sixteen."

Anna was speechless. Tears welled up in her eyes. She realized nothing she said at that moment would be good enough.

"I was two weeks shy of my 18th birthday when the couple I was with adopted me," Meg continued. "I have been with my parents for four years. They changed my life. My grades improved and I made up for the years I had lost. I graduated from high school a year later than my peers but with respectable grades."

"These parents don't mind you are living like a nomad?" Cassie asked.

Meg had come to Dolphin Bay as a tourist. She had told Cassie she was taking her time exploring the California coast.

"I decided to take a gap year before going to college," Meg explained. "I wanted to find my birth parents if possible. My parents, I mean, my adoptive parents, understand that."

"Why are you still called Meg Butler?" Cassie asked. "That's the name on your birth certificate but I thought the people adopting you would give you their name."

"It's the name in the records, I guess," Meg shrugged. "No one changed it. The foster families called me by any name they wanted. Megan, Margaret, Margie…no one really cared or remembered. By the time I got adopted again, I was so used to being Meg Butler, my parents decided to keep it."

"It worked in our favor," Anna said. "I am sure it made it easier for you to track us down."

"How exactly did you track us down?" Cassie asked again, pointing her fork at Meg.

"It wasn't easy," Meg replied. "Then I got a lucky break."

Anna had a fair idea of what Meg meant by that. A few months ago, after John died and Anna got sick, she had taken a decision. She didn't want to die without meeting her granddaughter. So she had done some online research and come across websites that helped adopted children find their birth parents or families. She had posted her information on a few such websites with a personal note to her granddaughter. She was sure Meg had found her on one of those sites.

"Why didn't you just pick up the phone and call?" Cassie asked.

Meg looked a bit embarrassed.

"I wasn't sure …"

"You wanted to check us out," Cassie pounced. "Make sure we were worthy of you."

"That's not what I meant," Meg said, her cheeks turning pink with emotion.

She turned to Anna and waved at the table.

"This food is delicious. You didn't have to go to all this effort."

"It was nothing, sweetie," Anna assured her. "I didn't know what you like. I use a lot of different stuffings for my ravioli but I just stuck with cheese for tonight."

"I'm not a picky eater."

"What's for dessert?" Cassie asked, interrupting them.

Anna told her to get the tiramisu from the refrigerator. Meg was quiet as they ate dessert. Anna thought she was trying to drum up the courage to say something.

"Why did you give me up?" Meg asked suddenly.

Anna was surprised to see there was no anger or malice in Meg's voice. She just stared at Cassie curiously. Anna thought it was the most natural question Meg could ask her mother.

Cassie put her fork down and wiped her mouth. She took her time thinking over the question.

"I was too young. I didn't think I could take care of you."

"Is that all?"

"I was sixteen when I gave birth to you, Meg. I was still in high school. I didn't have a job or any money."

"What about my father? Did he not want me too?"

Anna swallowed a lump as she heard Meg speak. She wanted to reach out and hold Meg tight. She had failed her grandchild. She and John should have taken a stronger stand and never let Cassie give her up.

"I thought you would have a better life," Cassie shrugged. "At least, better than the one I could give you."

They all knew how that had turned out for Meg. Anna marveled at how composed the young girl was. Why wasn't she lashing out at them?

Meg held Cassie's gaze and gave her a smile.

"I forgive you."

Chapter 6

Anna started baking as soon as she finished her coffee the next morning. She didn't realize how late it was until the Firecrackers arrived.

Anna set a plate of freshly baked cupcakes before her friends. Julie and Mary didn't waste a minute in picking one up.

"What batch is this?" Mary asked, daintily licking frosting off a cake. "I like the strong thyme flavor."

"This is the 11th batch," Anna said. "Let me make a note of that."

She scribbled something in a tiny notebook she pulled out of a kitchen drawer.

Julie was reaching for her second cupcake.

"I'm sorry I wasn't here yesterday. I had a deadline. It was midnight by the time I sent the files over to my editor."

"That's okay," Anna said. "You can't stop working every time I have a crisis. I seem to have so many of them."

"Well, I'm here now," Julie said. "What's the plan?"

"Yes," Mary nodded. "What are we doing today, Anna, other than tasting these yummy cupcakes?"

"I've been on edge since yesterday," Anna confessed. "Ever since Gino said the police see me as a suspect, I jump at every little sound. I expect them to come and take me away any time."

"Why would you kill a perfect stranger?" Mary asked.

"Yeah." Julie backed her up. "What is your connection with the dead guy?"

"That's just it," Anna muttered. "I don't exactly remember. He did some work here a few years ago. I can't do any better than that."

"And you say Lara Crawford's making a big deal out of it?"

Anna had told them Lara's theory about the dead guy being a witness to John's death.

"We need to find out more about him," Mary spoke up. "Do you even know his name?"

"I wrote it down somewhere," Anna said. She looked around for the small notepad she kept by the phone and found it in the utensil drawer. "William Parker. I think that's it."

"Didn't you say he was a handyman?" Julie asked. "He should be in the yellow pages."

Anna opened the pantry door and lugged a couple of giant tomes from the bottom shelf. She handed one to Julie and Mary and kept one for herself. They began rifling through the pages. Julie looked up a few minutes later.

"I don't see him under Handyman."

"Wait a minute," Anna exclaimed. "I think he's listed under roofing. Look at this, Dolphin Bay Roof Repair. The proprietor is listed as one William Parker."

"Do you see an address?" Julie asked eagerly.

"I know this place!" Anna exclaimed. "It's that small business park near the highway. It's about four miles from here."

Julie jumped down from her stool and slung her bag over her shoulder.

"What are we waiting for, ladies? Let's go!"

"Why are we going there, Julie?" Mary asked.

"We'll find out when we get there," Julie replied.

"That's right," Anna agreed.

Julie drove them to the business park in her SUV. It was a square, industrial type building nestled in a cluster of towering pines and eucalyptus. An automatic glass door slid open as the ladies walked in, looking around curiously. A massive wooden desk graced the center of the lobby and was presided over by a stern, bespectacled woman.

"May I help you?" she asked curtly.

Julie took the lead.

"We are looking for Dolphin Bay Roof Repair."

"They closed down six months ago," the woman replied. "Will that be all?"

"Are you sure they aren't around?" Julie asked, placing her arms on the counter. "They come highly recommended. William Parker did some work for one of my friends and she swears by him. I really wanted to get an estimate from him."

The woman behind the counter leaned forward.

"They had a big falling out, him and his partner. The business shut down after that."

"What were they fighting over?" Julie asked.

"I don't know," the woman said with a shrug.

She picked up the phone and began dialing a number. Julie gave up and walked to the door, followed by Anna and Mary.

"That didn't take long!" Anna said.

"It was a waste of time," Julie grumbled.

"Not really," Anna said thoughtfully. "We now know William Parker had a partner he didn't get along with. We need to track this guy down."

"Not before lunch!" Julie announced. "I'm starving."

"I saw you eat three cupcakes," Mary said meekly.

"That was ages ago!"

"Okay, okay, calm down." Anna tried to be the peacemaker. "Let's go to the Tipsy Whale."

The Tipsy Whale was the local pub and watering hole. The owner Murphy was well known for his giant, overstuffed sandwiches.

The pub was packed when they got there. They decided to get the sandwiches to go.

"Why don't we take these to the gazebo?" Mary asked. "It's a beautiful day to be out in the sun."

"I got the day's special," Julie said, waving the large paper bag. "It's rotisserie chicken with sweet peppers, avocadoes and secret sauce. Murphy hasn't made these in a while."

"Did you get the taro chips?" Anna asked.

"You bet I did!" Julie crowed.

The three friends walked over to a small green patch that cut right through Main Street. The rustic gazebo that sat in the center was the pride of the town. Covered in blue and purple wisteria blooms and freshly painted white for the summer season, it provided a welcoming space for the locals.

Anna took a few bites of her sandwich and put it down. Her appetite wasn't that great after her illness.

"How are we going to search for the partner?"

Julie set her sandwich down, wiped her hands on a napkin and pulled out her rose gold computer tablet from her bag.

She never went anywhere without it.

"I had an idea while driving back," she told the others. "What would a roofing contractor do if he closed down one business?"

"Stop talking in riddles," Anna grumbled. "What's your point?"

"I mean, this guy must be working as a handyman or roofer somewhere else."

"But we don't even know his name!" Anna protested.

"We can call up the people we find and ask them if they knew William Parker," Julie said.

She tapped some keys on her computer and muttered to herself as she read off the screen.

"Aha!" she exclaimed. "This guy has thirty years of experience and previously owned Dolphin Bay Roof Repair."

"What's his name?" Anna asked eagerly. "Anyone we know?"

"I don't think so." Julie shook her head. "Tim Buckner. Ever heard of him?"

Anna took the tablet from Julie's hand and began reading off the screen.

"Buckner and Sons, Roofing Contractors, Blackberry Beach. No job too small. Thirty years experience running own roofing business in Dolphin Bay."

She looked up with a smile.

"You're right, Julie. This looks like our guy."

"Blackberry Beach is what, twenty-twenty five miles from here? Maybe this guy still lives here in town."

"Should we call him right away?" Anna asked.

Her phone rang before Julie could answer. Anna listened for a minute, thanked the caller and hung up.

"That was the police," she said, looking excited. "They are done with the store. I can open it whenever I want."

Mary and Julie both cheered.

"Let's get over there and see what state the place is in," Julie said.

"We are going to need a thorough clean up," Mary warned.

Bayside Books, Anna's store, was situated at one end of Main Street. It barely took them ten minutes to walk over. A deputy from the local police was standing on the sidewalk outside the store. He left after Anna gave everything a quick onceover.

Mary was already pulling out the vacuum cleaner from a closet. Anna looked around at the dust on the furniture and the muddy footprints littering the floor. She avoided going into the new section where they had found William Parker.

"Hold on a second, Mary," she said. "This is too much work for us. I think I am going to call a cleaning service."

"Good idea," Julie echoed.

She wasn't too fond of elbow grease, especially her own.

The old fashioned bell behind the door jingled and a tall, attractive young girl came in. Anna decided her hazel eyes were her most beautiful feature. The girl flashed a wide smile at the women and greeted them.

"Hello! Are you open? I just wanted to pick up the latest bestseller."

"Which one?" Anna asked.

"I don't care," the girl laughed. "I'll read anything, really. I just need something to read before I fall asleep."

"Are you new in town?" Anna asked as she handed over a book to the girl and rang up her purchase.

"Sort of," the girl said. "I'm just visiting."

"I'm Anna Butler," Anna offered. "This is my store."

"I'm Ashley," the girl replied. "It's nice to meet you, Anna."

Chapter 7

Cassie woke up with a start. It was mid-morning and the sun was climbing high in the sky. She had been napping by the pool, wearing a flimsy kimono over her bikini. Her skin was a bit sore from the extra dose of sunshine she had subjected it to the previous day. She had been dreaming she was on set, trying to give the same shot for 15 takes. She kept forgetting her lines. It was the stuff of nightmares for an actress of Cassie's caliber.

Cassie called Bobby, eager to tell him about the horrific dream. Bobby listened sympathetically and consoled her.

"You've been gone too long, babe," he cried. "That's what this dream means. You need to get yourself back here, back where it matters."

"I can't, Bobby. At least not yet."

Cassie complained about the nagging pain in her knee. Bobby warned her to do her exercises diligently. They gossiped for some time and then Bobby had to go meet his next client.

Cassie had heard Anna and her friends discussing something at the top of their voices earlier. The house seemed quiet suddenly and she assumed they had gone out. She thought of the previous evening. Dinner with Meg hadn't been as awkward as she feared it would be. She hadn't said much to the young girl, letting Anna do most of the talking. She still found it hard to believe that Meg was her daughter.

She thought back to when she had met Meg for the first time. Meg had been going by the name Rain. Cassie had been drawn to the young girl, thinking there was something very familiar about her. She had been shocked when they accidentally discovered who Meg was.

On an impulse, Cassie dialed Meg's number. Meg answered immediately and agreed to come over. Fifteen minutes later, the doorbell rang. Cassie opened it a bit apprehensively, sipping a tall icy glass of lemonade.

"Fancy a swim?" she asked Meg. "You can borrow one of my bathing suits. I think we are the same size."

"Maybe later. Is Anna here?"

"Mom's gone out with the Firecrackers."

"Huh?"

"Julie and Mary, her friends. I don't know who came up with the name but the three of them christened themselves 'firecrackers' since before I was born."

Meg smiled. "It suits them."

"Let me get you some lemonade."

Cassie trooped into the kitchen and Meg followed her quietly. She accepted the cool drink her mother offered and took a long sip.

"What did you want to talk about, Cassie?"

Cassie hesitated. She walked into the living room and sat on the couch, pulling her legs up and tucking them under her. Meg sat opposite her.

Neither of them said anything for a while. Meg was the first to break the silence.

"You don't need to tell anyone."

Cassie sat up a bit straighter.

"I am not here to make your life difficult. I just needed to see where I came from."

Cassie hadn't given a thought yet to what she would tell the neighbors or the townsfolk. Was Anna planning to introduce Meg as her granddaughter?

"And what do you think? Are we good enough for you?"

"It's not like that, Cassie." Meg sighed. "Being a foster kid, you always wonder."

"You must hate me a lot. I am the villain who abandoned you, gave you up to a stranger."

"All that's water under the bridge. No use going over it now."

"What do you want from us now? Are you planning to come live here in Dolphin Bay?"

"I don't know." Meg gave a shrug. "Frankly, I focused all

my energy on tracking you down. I haven't given much thought to what comes after."

"You have met me now," Cassie pointed out. "I think it's time you started thinking about your next move."

"Can we be friends?"

"I suppose there is no harm in that."

Cassie wondered if she sounded distant. She didn't want to.

"I don't blame you for what you did, Cassie," Meg burst out. "I am sure you had your reasons."

"I always thought you would be adopted in a nice family and have a normal life. That's what the sisters told me. I guess I was too naïve."

"Sisters?"

"When I got pregnant, Mom and I went away to a small town in the Midwest. We told people I had been accepted into an arts program for gifted kids. Actually, we stayed in a convent for six months."

"I was born in 1995. Being a teen mom might have been rare but surely it wasn't taboo? Not like in the 60s."

"I was ambitious, Meg. I had big dreams. A baby would have ruined my acting career before it started."

Meg was quiet while she digested Cassie's information. Cassie wondered if she should tell her how it had been. She was the one who had suggested going away. She had convinced her parents to keep her condition a secret.

"Did you hold me when I was born?"

Cassie swallowed a lump. Her memory was still vivid. She remembered the exact moment the crying, red faced baby had been placed in her arms. How many times had she relived that moment over the years?

"I chose your name," she said emotionally. "You are named after Meg Ryan. She was famous in the 90s."

"I know who Meg Ryan is, Cassie."

"I was obsessed with Meg. She was my role model, you know. I wanted to be just like her. I made sure they called you Meg. It's not short for anything. It's just Meg."

"What about my father? Does he know about me?"

Cassie pursed her lips. "No."

Meg looked disappointed.

"I'm sorry to tell you this, but I don't know who your father is."

"How is that possible? I am guessing he was someone who lived here in Dolphin Bay. Someone you went to school with."

Cassie didn't know what to say. Even after all these years, she wasn't sure she could defend her actions.

"I was in love with a local boy. My parents thought I was

too young to be serious about anyone. They turned out to be right. We got into a big fight one day and broke up. I sneaked off to a party and ..."

Cassie didn't know how to continue. She had been angry enough to hook up with some random guy at the party. She didn't exactly remember what had happened that night.

Meg folded her arms and looked at her stonily.

"A few weeks later, I realized I was pregnant," Cassie told her. "I left town and went to Los Angeles after you were born. I never really came back home."

Cassie tried to gauge Meg's reaction. Was she angry, shocked or disappointed?

"At least I found you," Meg murmured.

"Have you had lunch?" Cassie asked impulsively, trying to diffuse the tension. "Why don't we go get a bite to eat?"

Meg gave a shrug but said nothing.

"Give me a few minutes, Meg. I'll be out in a jiffy."

Ten minutes later, Cassie came out of her room, dressed in faded jeans and a white crop top. She was wearing another Hermes scarf from her collection and a cloud of her favorite Joy perfume surrounded her as she nodded at Meg.

Meg's eyes were red. With a pang, Cassie realized the young girl had been crying in her absence.

"I hope you like your meat!" she said cheerfully. "The

Yellow Tulip makes a mean cheeseburger."

Cassie's phone trilled before Meg could answer.

"Hello? Yes, this is Cassie Butler."

She listened to the voice at the other end.

"Thank you for thinking of me, darling, but I can't get away right now. I'm still needed here at home." She blew an air kiss before saying 'ciao' and hung up.

Meg was quiet while Cassie started her car. The ancient Mercedes convertible started after three tries. Cassie sped off with a screech of tires and parked at the corner of Main Street five minutes later. The Downtown Loop was a two mile zone which was off limits to cars.

They walked to the Yellow Tulip Diner and snagged a booth toward the far end. The waitress came to take their orders. Cassie ordered cheese burgers and crinkle cut fries for the both of them along with the root beer floats the diner was famous for.

"I'm not that hungry," Meg said.

"You will be once you start eating. Aren't you kids supposed to have a hearty appetite?"

Meg toyed with the salt and pepper shakers on the table.

"I wonder what Mom's up to," Cassie said, trying to think of a neutral topic of conversation.

Her ears pricked up at the raised voices coming from the

adjoining booth.

"William Parker was scum. I am not sorry he is dead. I say he had it coming."

Chapter 8

Anna was making chicken piccata with linguine and mushroom risotto. She didn't think it was too much. Gino was coming to dinner and she wanted to be sure they had plenty of food. The wine was breathing on the counter and the salad was already made.

The doorbell rang and before Anna knew it, Gino came into the kitchen, holding a bottle of wine in his hands. He gave Anna a hug and kissed her on the cheek.

"What's the occasion?"

"Just friends having dinner. I owe you one after all those meals I mooched off you."

"Something smells good," Gino said, taking in a deep breath. "Where's Cassie?"

"Watching that infernal movie again. I think she must have watched Casablanca a thousand times."

"Casablanca! Really? It's my favorite too."

Anna rolled her eyes and stirred the risotto. It was almost done. She added in the grated parmesan cheese and pulled her apron off.

Twenty minutes later, they were enjoying the tasty meal Anna had produced.

"How's your sleuthing going?" Gino asked after he complimented Anna on the chicken.

"William Parker, the dead guy, had a feud with his partner. I tracked him down. He has a new business in the neighboring town but I have a hunch he still lives in Dolphin Bay."

"Let me guess. You are planning to go talk to him."

"As soon as I find out more about him. I had a doctor's appointment today so I had to put it off."

"Are you ill?" Gino asked with concern.

"Just routine follow-up," Anna replied coolly. "Nothing to worry about."

Anna urged Gino to try the roasted broccoli.

"I'm not a big fan," Gino confessed.

"What are you, ten?" Anna teased. "You gotta eat your greens."

Gino admitted the broccoli wasn't bad and moved to the risotto. His eyes lit up when he tasted the creamy dish. He paid complete attention to his food for a while. Anna sipped her wine, watching him with a smug smile. Cooking was one thing she was good at.

"You know what's bothering me most about this thing?" Gino asked, serving himself some more risotto. "What was this dead guy doing in your store? He either died there or he was brought there after he was killed. But why your store, Anna?"

"I have wondered about it too. I have a wild idea. Do you think Lara Crawford had something to do with this? She's going around telling people I am involved in the guy's death, right? What if she set the whole thing up?"

"Are you saying she killed this William Parker? Even Lara wouldn't go that far."

"You think so?" Anna muttered.

"I don't like her any more than you do, Anna. But she is the mayor of this town. She is a respectable citizen and what's more, she doesn't have any motive."

"And I do?"

"Calm down. That's not what I meant."

"I wouldn't put anything past her."

"Don't let prejudice cloud your judgment, Anna. You don't want to fall in the same trap as her."

Anna grudgingly admitted to herself that Gino was right.

"What about that guy who was hounding you to sell the store? Do you think he might be behind this?"

"Jose Garcia? He's living it up in Cabo. And the store's not a problem now. I have a lease on the adjoining store for as long as I want. You haven't seen the renovations yet so you don't know. We knocked a wall down and it's one giant space now. Although I think I will keep the two entrances.

That way, people who just want to go to the café don't have to troop through the bookstore."

"How did you manage the lease?" Gino asked curiously.

"Julie came to my rescue. She bought the store and leased it to me for the next twenty years. I will probably be long gone by then."

"Surely not!" Gino said. "You are very fortunate to have friends like Julie."

"Don't I know it?"

Anna had already decided she would give a percentage of the café profits to Julie. Of course, that could only happen when the café was up and running and actually making profit. She crossed her fingers and hoped it would happen soon.

Cassie came into the kitchen and greeted Gino.

"I hope you saved some dinner for me."

"Your food's cold," Anna chided, pointing to a covered plate. "Why are you late, Cassie? I thought you knew we had company."

"I was giving you two some alone time."

Anna turned red. Gino couldn't hide a grin.

"When are you taking my Mom out on a proper date?"

"Whenever she says yes," Gino said with a twinkle in his

eyes.

"You haven't asked me yet, Gino Mancini," Anna quipped.

Gino leaned forward and looked into Anna's eyes.

"What is your answer going to be?"

"You won't know until you ask."

"Charlie Robinson's already invited her for lunch at the resort," Cassie offered, cutting into her lemony chicken. "I say you have some stiff competition there."

"I think you were better off watching that movie," Anna grumbled.

"What were you two talking about, Mom?"

Gino stopped smiling.

"We were trying to figure out what a dead guy's doing in your mother's bookstore."

"Oh, yeah!" Cassie exclaimed. "I totally forgot what happened yesterday, Mom."

She told them about her visit to the diner.

"You know how that waitress at the Yellow Tulip likes to talk? I didn't have to work too hard to get some information out of her."

"Go on," Anna said, pushing her plate away.

"It's a bit too fantastic. It seems William Parker did a

number on this guy."

"Was she more specific?" Gino asked sharply.

"This guy was William Parker's customer. William Parker had an affair with his wife. And that's not all. She got pregnant and actually gave birth to the child."

"What is this man's name? Is he anyone we know?" Anna asked.

"Ethan Lapin. Youngish chap with blonde hair and a broken nose."

"Doesn't ring a bell," Anna said.

"He's an EMT here in Dolphin Bay," Cassie told them. "Lives with his wife and kids."

"Are you saying this Ethan wanted to have revenge?" Gino asked. "It sounds like a motive alright."

"We need to find out more about him," Anna said eagerly. "I will go talk to him."

"Please be careful, Anna. I can go with you if you want."

"I'll have the girls with me," Anna assured him. "Now, how about some dessert? We have strawberry cheesecake."

"I couldn't eat another bite," Gino said, placing a hand on his stomach. "But I can't say no to dessert."

Anna got up to bring the cake out. Cassie cornered Gino.

"Can you run a background check for me?"

"Sure. Is someone bothering you, Cassie?"

"Not really. I just want to make sure this person is who they say they are."

"Tell me more." Gino folded his hands and leaned back in his chair.

"What are you two talking about?" Anna asked as she came out with a large cheesecake smothered in strawberry compote and fresh strawberries.

She placed it on the table and cut three generous slices.

Cassie gave Gino a warning glance. Anna saw her.

"What are you hiding, Cassie?"

Cassie gave a dramatic sigh. "I want to run a background check on Meg. I was asking Gino if he could do it for me."

"Isn't that the young girl who is helping you out at the store, Anna?" Gino asked. "Don't you trust her?"

"I do," Anna said, the same time as Cassie stated she didn't.

"Neither of you are making any sense." Gino took a big bite of the cheesecake and kissed his fingers. "This is delicious, Anna. I'm going to be lining up every day when you open the café."

"I trust Meg," Anna said.

"We don't know anything about her, Mom," Cassie said. "I can't just believe everything she says."

"Get a DNA test," Anna blurted out.

"DNA test?" Gino's eyebrows shot up. "Who is this girl, exactly?"

Cassie gave Gino the Cliff Notes version of how Meg was related to them. Gino rubbed his hand over his head.

"There's never a dull moment with you two. So this girl Meg turns up and says she is your daughter. Anna believes her but you don't. What exactly do you want me to find out, Cassie?"

"Is she really the child I gave up for adoption?"

"That's a tough task, Cassie. It's going to take time. I think Anna's right. The quickest and surest way to find out is have a DNA test."

Anna wondered how long it would take Cassie to come around.

"I want to be reasonably sure who she is before I go in for a test," Cassie protested. "She could just be conning us, Mom. I think she just read your message on that website and decided you were an easy target. An emotional old woman, reasonably well off, living by herself. She saw an opportunity and took it."

"I'm sorry, Anna, but Cassie does have a point. I have seen many cases of crooks preying on vulnerable old people."

"For shame, Cassie," Anna cried. "How can you be so callous?"

She dabbed her eyes with a tissue and squared her shoulders.

"You can run any checks you want, Cassie. Sooner or later, you will have to accept that Meg is your daughter. I just hope you don't drive her away in the process."

Chapter 9

Anna sat in her garden the next morning, sipping coffee and thinking about Gino. He had helped her load the dishwasher after Cassie left them alone the previous night. They had come out in the garden and sat on the park bench under the climbing rose, enjoying the balmy summer evening. Anna had enjoyed talking with him, long after the sun set and the twilight gave way to a starry sky. Gino had told her about his kids and how much he missed them. Anna told him about her illness and how she was coping. The evening had ended on a bittersweet note, both of them reluctant to bid each other good night.

Cassie came out of the house, gripping a large mug of coffee in both hands. She nodded at Anna through swollen eyes.

"I have the worst headache, Mom."

"Were you drinking last night?"

"What? No. What makes you say that?"

"I know all about your habits, Cassie. Don't lie to me."

"I might have had a nightcap," Cassie conceded. "Or two."

"You need to deal with this, honey," Anna pleaded. "Meg is here to stay. You will have to accept it."

"What do you mean, stay?" Cassie asked, alarmed. "She's not going to live in this house?"

"Maybe not yet, but eventually. This is where she belongs."

"This is too much on an empty stomach. I need to eat, Mom. Did you throw away my frosted flakes again?"

Anna stood up with a sigh.

"Avocado toast is much healthier. Do you want omelets or poached eggs to go with it?"

"Anything's fine," Cassie mumbled, stifling a yawn.

Anna went inside and slid four slices of bread in the toaster. She cut two ripe avocadoes and started mashing them. They sat down to eat five minutes later.

Anna poured hot sauce over her toast and looked at Cassie.

"What are you doing today? Do you want to go with me?"

"Where to?"

"I want to check out where William Parker lives."

"What about Aunt Julie and Aunt Mary?"

"Julie's on a deadline and Mary's got a meeting of the Garden Club."

"I am expecting a call from my agent," Cassie said.

"You don't have to be home for that." Anna didn't comment on Cassie's favorite excuse. "Get ready. We are

72

leaving in fifteen minutes."

Cassie didn't know how Anna had obtained William Parker's address. They drove to an older part of town. One of Cassie's friends from high school had lived in the area and she vaguely remembered it. The house was old and run down and in much need of repair.

"Wasn't he supposed to be a handyman?" Cassie asked Anna. "How did he not take care of his own house?"

"He might have been too busy fixing other people's homes," Anna shrugged.

She had to admit the Parker residence was an eyesore. It was a small ranch style bungalow on a large wooded lot. The grass was knee high and the path leading up to the house was covered in weeds. Wildflowers bloomed everywhere, giving the place a rustic charm.

Cassie took the lead and walked up the rickety steps leading to a porch. She pressed the small bell she discovered next to a screen door. She waited for a couple of minutes and started banging on the door with her hand.

"I don't think anyone's home, Cassie."

A woman came out of a house two doors down and waved at them. She was holding a sniffling toddler in her arms.

"That place is empty now," she told them. "Were you looking for Handyman Bill?"

Anna nodded.

"He died," she said, placing a hand over the child's ears. "It was in the Chronicle."

"We wanted to pay our respects," Anna said, holding out the casserole she had brought with her as cover. "He did some jobs for us over the years. He was a good worker."

"Oh, I hope you didn't come a long way. It was just him."

"What about his family?"

"Never saw any. We just moved here six months ago. You might want to talk to old Bertha." She pointed at a door on the other side of the street. "She's been here forever. And she's a busybody. Knows everything that goes on here."

The toddler began to wail. The woman wished them luck and went inside.

"She might have offered us a drink," Cassie complained. "It's too hot to be out in the sun."

Anna ignored her daughter and began walking toward Bertha's house. It was a small Cape Cod with a fresh coat of paint and a meticulously kept garden. The door opened before she lifted her hand to knock. Anna found herself looking at a well dressed woman around her own age.

"Hello. I saw you peeping into William Parker's house. Were you friends with that scoundrel?"

Anna realized she needed to change her cover story.

"William Parker was found dead in my bookstore. I was hoping to meet some of his family."

The woman's eyes sparkled with interest.

"So you are the one the whole town is talking about. If you killed him, you did us all a big favor."

Anna took Cassie's arm and smiled at the woman.

"This is my daughter, Cassandra Butler. You might remember seeing her in the movies."

That did it. Anna watched with amusement as the woman fawned all over Cassie. She ushered them into the house and plied them with cake and lemonade. It was a while before Anna could get a word in.

"I'm assuming you didn't like your neighbor much."

Bertha snorted.

"That man was scum, let me tell you. His family thought so too. That's why none of them stuck around."

"Oh?" Anna quirked an eyebrow and leaned forward slightly, inviting Bertha to go on.

"His wife was the first one to go. I think the poor woman just couldn't take it anymore. He cheated on her openly, you know. And I think he beat her too. She finally had the sense to leave."

Anna hadn't expected that.

"Did he have any kids?"

"The kids went off to college and never came back. I think

there was a son who looked in on him about once a year. He wanted the son to come and live here, take care of the business. Obviously, that didn't happen."

Anna asked about the partner. Bertha had never heard of him.

"Did he have many visitors?"

Bertha topped up Cassie's glass with more lemonade and shook her head.

"Not that I know of."

"Did you see anyone suspicious hanging around recently? Or see him talking to anyone new?"

Bertha's brows settled in a frown.

"Now that you mention it, I do think someone was following him. I saw the same car parked by the side of the road a couple of times. William noticed it too. He came out of the house and tapped on the window."

"Was it someone he knew?"

Bertha gave a shrug.

"The man in the car got out and said something. William must have lost his temper. He was screaming at the man, waving his arms around. I couldn't hear them but I think he was threatening the man in the car."

"What happened after that?" Anna asked, holding her breath. "Did they hit each other?"

Bertha shook her head.

"The man got into the car and drove away. I didn't see the car back here again."

"When did all this happen?" Anna asked.

"About two or three days before they found him," Bertha said.

Anna pulled out her business card from her bag and handed it to Bertha.

"Can you please call me if you remember anything else?"

"What are you, some kind of modern Miss Marple?"

"You know what the people are saying?" Anna asked. "I'm just trying to help myself."

"Smart move," Bertha nodded approvingly. "I would do the same."

Anna nudged Cassie as they walked out. Cassie turned around and thanked Bertha. Bertha pulled out a DVD from a shelf and made Cassie autograph it.

"That went well." Anna smiled as Cassie pressed her foot on the gas pedal.

"Do you think we have another suspect, Mom?"

"Sure looks like it, sweetie."

"Where do you want to go now?"

"Let's have lunch in town. What do you feel like eating?"

"Wonton soup and Hunan Chicken."

"China Garden it is," Anna nodded. "I'm craving some Lo Mein noodles and shrimp myself."

A large, noisy group of women was already seated when they entered the Chinese restaurant. Anna spotted Mary among the women.

"The Garden Club decided to have lunch here," Mary whispered as she got up and gave Anna a hug.

"Are you still discussing the Rose Show?" Anna asked with interest.

"The meeting spilled over," Mary nodded. "A few members suggested we should go big this year. They are proposing we accept entries from the neighboring counties. But the old guard is against that. We are still going to and fro over it. It's going to be hard to reach any consensus."

"Good luck with that, Mary. What is your stance?"

"The more, the merrier. It's a great fund raising opportunity for the club."

A loud, imperious voice broke into their conversation, startling them.

"What do you think you are doing, Mary?" Agnes, the head of the Rose Show Committee demanded. "Are you talking about club business with that murderer?"

Chapter 10

Cassie laced up her sneakers and checked herself in the mirror. Birds were chirping outside her window and a light mist hung over the early morning. Cassie had come up with a plan while she binged on some old movies the previous night. She knew that Teddy Fowler, the detective, went for a run on the Coastal Walk every morning. She planned to meet him accidentally and get him talking. Teddy had a loose tongue and an inclination to boast about his work.

Anna nodded toward a glass of orange juice as soon as Cassie stepped out of her room.

"Freshly squeezed, just for you."

"You didn't have to, Mom. Thanks."

Cassie sipped some of the juice and asked Anna about her plans for the day.

"I'm making blueberry pancakes for breakfast. I hope you work up an appetite."

"Don't worry, I will."

Cassie walked toward the Coastal Walk and started jogging toward the sprawling castle like building at the far end. She picked up her pace after a while and didn't slow down until she reached the Castle Beach Resort. She flopped down on an empty bench that offered a spectacular view of the bay.

"Howdy!" a familiar voice greeted her.

Cassie waved at Teddy and patted the spot next to her.

"Take a load off, Teddy. There's plenty of room here."

Teddy sprawled on the bench, panting from the exertion. Cassie waited until his breathing returned to normal.

"Nice day. How's it going, Teddy?"

"I can't talk about it, Cassie, but you know I'm working on the latest murder."

"Do you mean that guy they found in our store? That's a tough one."

"I call it a slam dunk."

"How so?" Cassie asked innocently. "There are so many suspects, it's hard to say who's guilty."

"Of course you would say that," Teddy countered. "Your mother's the guilty one, Cassie."

"From what I've heard, that guy was hated by one and all. Too many people had a motive to kill him, Teddy."

"I don't agree. As far as I am concerned, your mother has the biggest motive. He knew something incriminating about her and so she silenced him. It's as simple as that."

"That's a load of nonsense, Teddy."

"Everyone in town is talking about it, Cassie."

Cassie tried to control her anger. She didn't want to upset Teddy.

"What kind of detective are you? You can't believe something just because the gossip mongers are saying it."

"Come on, Cassie. I have solid information. I can't tell you everything the police are privy to."

"Are you talking about the autopsy report?" Cassie asked him. "What does it say about the cause of death?"

"Look, Cassie," Teddy sighed. "The timing is highly suspicious. Don't you see? This guy dies right after we reopen the investigation in your father's death. He witnessed something at that time and Anna had to silence him."

Cassie shook her head.

"You are wrong."

"Forget about all this. When are you coming to dinner? My wife wants to know."

"You've got some nerve," Cassie huffed. "You think I'm going to come to your house after listening to all that rot about my mother?"

"I'm just doing my job, Cassie!"

Cassie stood up without a word and started jogging away from Teddy, ignoring his pleas to stop and hear him out. She was exhausted by the time she got home.

"What's the matter?" Anna's eyes shot up in alarm when she looked at Cassie's defiant expression.

"Teddy thinks you are guilty. It's like he doesn't have a mind of his own."

"Forget about that for now and come eat."

Anna stood over a towering stack of fluffy pancakes bursting with blueberries. She fixed a plate for Cassie and urged her to calm down.

"Our problems aren't going anywhere, sweetie."

"I know that," Cassie said, generously pouring maple syrup over her pancakes. "I'm going to meet Aunt Mary. I have a job for her."

"You do that," Anna nodded.

"What are your plans for the day? Aren't you going to open the bookstore?"

"The cleaning crew isn't done yet," Anna replied. "And the workmen are doing some last minute stuff in the café portion."

"So you can join me and Aunt Mary?"

"Actually, I made some other plans."

Cassie frowned, giving Anna a suspicious look.

"What could be more important than this, Mom? Don't you realize how serious this is? The police might arrest you any moment."

"You're stressing too much," Anna dismissed.

Cassie poured a little syrup over the last remaining piece of pancake and speared it with her fork.

"What are you hiding, Mom?" Her face crumpled suddenly and she looked at Anna in dismay. "Are you feeling alright? Do we need to go to the doctor?"

"I just had a doctor's appointment, thank you very much. And what have I told you about coddling me, Cassie?"

"I worry about you, Mom. We all do. Now tell me what's wrong."

"Nothing!" Anna snapped. "Meg's coming here for breakfast. We are going out after that."

Cassie felt a stab of jealousy.

"Out?"

"I'm taking her shopping, okay? We might drive to some outlet malls or go up to San Francisco."

Cassie realized they had planned a whole day without her. But she couldn't really blame them after the cold reception she had given Meg.

"Sorry I asked!"

"I just want to spend some time with my granddaughter."

"I hope you enjoy yourself, Mom. I mean it."

Cassie went to her room and dialed Mary's number. Mary appeared thrilled to hear from her.

"Aren't you going to San Francisco?"

So the Firecrackers already knew about Anna and Meg's impending trip, Cassie realized.

"I have bigger fish to fry, Aunt Mary. You are friends with that medical examiner, aren't you?"

"You mean Rory Cunningham? He's more my husband's friend than mine."

"You think you can pick his brain?"

Cassie explained what she wanted to know.

"I don't know, Cassie. He's a busy man."

"Mom says he's partial to your banana cream pie."

"Are you putting me to work, young lady?"

Cassie knew Mary was just kidding. She would gladly bend over backwards if it meant helping Anna.

"Why don't we all meet for lunch at the Tipsy Whale?" Cassie suggested. "The man's gotta eat, right?"

Mary promised to get back to Cassie and hung up.

Cassie heard some voices out in the kitchen and figured Meg must have arrived while she was on the phone. She curbed her curiosity and stayed in her room. Anna knocked on her door a while later to tell her they were leaving.

"Drive safely, and bring me some salt water taffy from Fisherman's Wharf."

Cassie waited until she heard the front door close. She gave them a few more minutes before venturing out in the living room. Mary called to confirm their lunch appointment.

Cassie had a couple of hours on her hands. She changed into her bikini and headed out to the pool. Twenty laps later, the clanging in her head still hadn't abated. Cassie settled into her favorite cabana and wondered if Gino had made any progress running a background check on Meg. Was it too early to ask him for an update?

The phone rang and Cassie's face finally broke into a smile.

"Hola Bobbykins," she crooned. "You're just what I need right now."

Bobby looked lean and mean, fresh out of the shower.

"One of my clients cancelled at the last minute. I'm free for the next thirty minutes."

Bobby had stuck with Cassie through some pretty bad times. She trusted him more than either of her ex-husbands. Tears welled up in her eyes as she stared at the familiar face on the screen.

"What's the matter, babe?"

"You'll never guess what has happened." Cassie wiped her

face with the back of her hand. "I need you here, Bobby. I can't talk about this on the phone."

"Is the IRS bothering you again, Cass? I thought you made a deal with them?"

Cassie's tears were flowing freely.

"You're scaring me now, Cassie. Get a hold of yourself."

Cassie had kept her secret for twenty years. There was only one person she had trusted with it, only one person who had held her hand through long sleepless nights when she questioned the decision she had made as a child.

"I don't know what to do, Bobby. Will you please help me?"

"Hang on! I'm taking the next flight out. Just hang on, sweetie."

Cassie hung up, thankful she had a friend she could count on. She needed to talk to someone about Meg, someone who wasn't related to the young girl who was supposed to be her biological daughter.

Chapter 11

Meg walked on the beach, thinking about the last few days of her life.

Things had moved fast and she was still reeling a bit from the recent developments. When she set off on her trip to California, she had warned herself not to have high hopes. Shuffled from one foster home to another all her life, Meg was used to life letting her down. Getting adopted at sixteen had been the one good thing that happened to her. It had restored her faith in humanity.

Meg didn't know exactly when she had decided to go find her birth parents or why. What did she hope to achieve by meeting someone who had given her away? But her adoptive parents had encouraged her. Her therapist had encouraged her. They thought it would give her the closure she needed to get on with her life. So Meg started her research. She added her name to certain online databases and searched websites that promised to unite adopted kids with their birth parents. She had struck gold a few months in.

Meg had seen Anna's message on one of the websites and decided to come watch her from a distance. Anna's enthusiasm and warmth had bowled her over. Maybe grandmothers were like that.

She was less sure about Cassie. Meg sensed her hesitation but she didn't blame her. Cassie had seemed like a cool person when she ran into her at the local university. She looked so young. Meg had been shocked when she learned Cassie was her birth mother.

Meg spotted a surf board embedded in the sand and walked toward it. Dolphin Bay had a well kept secret. Surf enthusiasts flocked to the small beach where the waves were big and the crowds small. Meg had spotted a flyer for surfing lessons at the Yellow Tulip Diner and signed up.

Two girls were standing near the surf board. One of them waved at Meg.

"Hello! Are you here for your lesson?"

Meg nodded, feeling a slight apprehension. Raised in the Midwest, she wasn't really a water baby.

"I think this was a mistake," she said. "Can I cancel now?"

The girl laughed and patted her arm.

"Don't be scared. You'll be riding those waves before you know it." She nodded at the other girl. "Ask her."

Meg couldn't stop staring at the tall, brown haired beautiful young girl. They were about the same age but she possessed a sophistication Meg found sorely lacking in herself. The girl surprised her by greeting her with a quick hug.

"Hi. I'm Ashley. I'm new to surfing too. This is just my third lesson and I'm having a blast. Trust me, you are going to love it."

Meg had to agree after a while. She barely noticed when the

hour was up. She was already paddling out in the water and standing up on the board by herself.

"Aren't you starving?" Ashley exclaimed. "Do you want to grab some lunch?"

The surfing instructor recommended a small shack half a mile down the beach.

"They are not fancy, but they do a mean fish and chips."

They thanked the instructor and set off toward the shack. Ashley chattered nonstop about how great everything was. The sky was a super shade of blue, the ocean was a beautiful turquoise, the waves were just right, and the water was awesome, neither too hot, nor too cold. Meg thought she was a very positive kind of person.

After a few minutes, Meg tuned Ashley out and thought of her shopping trip with Anna. They had driven into San Francisco the previous day and done a few touristy things. She had been tongue tied at first, not sure what Anna wanted to talk about. But Anna had coaxed her into opening up and speaking her mind. Anna had made it very clear how happy she was to have Meg in her life.

"I'm not letting you go now, not after it took me twenty years to find you."

Did that mean she had been searching for Meg all this time?

"We're here," Ashley's voice echoed in her ear. "Hello! You look lost. What are you thinking about, Meg? Is it some hot guy you met in town?"

Meg cracked a smile at that. Dating was the farthest thing on her mind right now.

The menu was simple. Beer battered fish, hand cut fries and coleslaw with blackberry cobbler for dessert. There were a few canisters of seasoning on the rustic wooden table. The server told them it was a choice of paprika, Cajun seasoning or Italian herbs.

Ashley grabbed the container of Cajun seasoning and sprinkled it liberally over her fish and fries. She dipped the fish in the garlic aioli and took a healthy bite. Meg watched in fascination as the young girl closed her eyes and moaned in delight.

"This is so good!"

Meg took a tentative bite. She was more of a meatloaf kind of girl.

"So, where are you from?" Ashley asked. "You don't look like a native."

"I grew up in the Midwest," Meg nodded. "Far away from the ocean."

"What brings you to our shores?"

"I took a gap year after high school. Thought I would see a bit of my country before heading off to college."

"Lucky you," Ashley said, licking the creamy aioli off her fingers. "I can't even think of college."

"You don't like books?" Meg asked tentatively.

"Music is my jam!" Ashley laughed. "When I was a kid, I dreamed of going to Juilliard. That's a big music school in New York."

"Were you that good?"

"I thought so," Ashley said without guile. "I was putting in the work."

"What happened?"

Ashley shrugged. Her eyes had hardened. Meg was surprised at the sudden change she saw come over her.

"My father died when I was 12. Life just went downhill after that."

"I'm sorry to hear that," Meg said, feeling uncomfortable. "What about your mom?"

Ashley sighed.

"She worked herself to death, poor thing. But it wasn't enough. By the time I was fourteen, I was working two jobs. School was never a priority."

"I was lucky that way," Meg confessed. "I was a bad student but my parents encouraged me every step of the way. They hired special tutors so I could graduate high school."

"They sound like keepers."

"Best thing that happened to me," Meg nodded, realizing how true that was.

She wasn't planning on telling this stranger the whole story. But her adoptive parents had literally changed her life.

"It's a different kind of love, isn't it?" Ashley said wistfully. "What you feel for your parents? You would do anything for them."

Meg nodded but didn't say a word.

Her life was too complicated at present. Cassie was her mother but she had no idea how she felt about her. She certainly didn't love her. Or did she? Should she? Was there some kind of eternal bond between them, forged by spending nine months in her womb?

"Do you live in Dolphin Bay?" she asked Ashley, shaking off her melancholy thoughts.

"Oh no!" Ashley said, popping the last piece of fish in her mouth. "I'm a visitor, just like you. I'm familiar with the area though. I grew up a hundred miles down the coast, in Monterey."

"And you are just learning surfing?"

"Kayaking's more my thing. And honestly, I have been too busy working my butt off."

Meg remarked on what a coincidence it was that they had both opted for a surfing lesson that day.

"Kismet!" Ashley said, drawing a line across her forehead. "Fate, you know. But now that I've met you, I'm not letting you off. You better add me to your friends list."

"I'd like that," Meg said shyly.

"So what do you do when you are not taking surfing lessons?"

"I have a job at the local bookstore."

"I think I know the place. I went there a couple of days ago. Are they renovating or something?"

Meg told her about the upcoming café.

"I can't cook to save my life."

Meg assured her she wouldn't be doing any cooking either. The girls chatted for a while more, devoured the blackberry cobbler and said goodbye to each other after exchanging phone numbers and Instagram handles.

Meg walked home, wondering if she should look in on Anna. They had planned to try on all the clothes they had bought on their shopping spree. Meg wondered where Cassie was. She didn't always get a positive vibe from her. Although they had declared an unspoken truce for Anna's sake, Meg was a bit wary of the woman.

Meg chided herself for thinking harshly of her own mother. She needed to give her some time to come around. Meg wasn't sure how she was supposed to behave until Cassie appeared to thaw a bit.

Would Cassie allow her to get close to Anna?

Chapter 12

Anna Butler was happy. Her trip to San Francisco with Meg had turned out to be better than she expected. They had both had a good time. At least she thought so if she was any judge of character. They had come home weighed down with shopping bags, pleasantly tired from their day out. Anna had urged Meg to stay for dinner and ordered pizza. Cassie had taken her plate to her room.

Anna was having a leisurely day. She had been walking on air all morning. She had started baking as soon as breakfast was over. Her orange thyme cupcakes had passed her exacting standards. They were going to be a big hit when the café opened.

"What are you doing at home, Mom?" Cassie asked as she came in from the patio.

She had spent the morning sunning herself by the pool. Anna gave her an indulgent look.

"Are you hungry? I haven't thought of lunch yet."

"Do we have any leftovers? I don't feel like going out to the pub or diner."

"There's some soup," Anna said. "But I'm not sure it will be enough for all of us."

"All of us?" Cassie frowned.

"Meg said she might swing by."

"Wasn't she here yesterday?"

Anna put down the pastry bag she was holding and glared at Cassie.

"So what? She can come here as often as she likes. I invited her."

"I think you should be a bit cautious, Mom."

"She is not going to pick my wallet, Cassie. Have some faith."

"What about your heart, Mom? Don't get too involved. Not until we know more about her."

"That again. Gino told me what you said to him. Going behind my back! I don't know what to do with you, Cassie."

"I'm just doing my due diligence. You would do the same if you hadn't been blinded by this kid. She's already got you wrapped around her little finger."

"What if she has? She's entitled."

Cassie rolled her eyes and pulled out a loaf of bread and some butter from the refrigerator. She started slicing the bread viciously, refusing to look at Anna.

"I'm making my special garlic bread. I think it should be enough along with the soup."

"With the fresh garlic and parsley?" Anna asked.

Cassie nodded.

"That's the only kind I make."

"Let me get you some parsley from the garden."

Anna wiped her hands on her apron and walked out. She took her time coming back. Cassie had already grated garlic into the soft butter. She chopped the fresh herbs and added them to the butter.

"Let's not fight, okay?" Anna said, switching on the oven while Cassie buttered the bread. "Tell me what you did yesterday."

"I thought you'd never ask. I met Aunt Mary and Rory Cunningham for lunch at the Tipsy Whale."

"Rory, the medical examiner? What was he doing having lunch with you?"

"I wanted to pick his brain about the dead guy."

"Did you?" Anna held her breath.

"Rory said this one was a bit odd. He is not really sure about the cause of death."

"Did he say where the man had been killed?"

Anna wanted to know if the man had died at the bookstore or had just been dumped there.

"It appears the man was poisoned," Cassie explained. "But he was also hit on the head. Rory said the timing was such that it is hard to say what happened first."

"He must have been poisoned first," Anna mused.

"We don't know that," Cassie shrugged. "Maybe he got hurt, then ate or drank something that was poisoned."

"I guess that's possible too."

They both looked at each other and sighed.

"Why is everything so complicated?" Anna cried. "This doesn't help my case, does it?"

"I'm sorry, Mom."

Anna pursed her mouth and began heating the soup. It seemed like there wasn't going to be any respite for her. Her phone dinged and her expression softened when she read the message that had come in.

"Meg's having lunch with someone. There's plenty of food now, Cassie. You won't have to share."

"Where is she?" Cassie asked curiously.

"On Surfer's Beach. Says she just made a new friend."

"Good for her," Cassie said sourly.

Anna ladled the minestrone soup into her favorite bright yellow soup bowls. She had bought them in Tuscany on a legendary trip she and John had taken to Europe.

Cassie placed the garlic bread on a plate, picked one up and bit into it.

"Do you remember what that woman Bertha told us?" she asked Anna. "We still need to find this man who was following William Parker."

"I know," Anna said. "But I have no idea where to start."

"Did he sound familiar to you?"

Anna shook her head.

"If he's an outsider, he must be staying somewhere in town."

"Blackberry Beach has more motels than we do. The only options we have are Castle Beach Resort which is very pricey or that motel near the highway."

"Don't forget people letting out a room in their house," Cassie pointed out. "Aunt Mary's one of them."

"Someone usually mentions something and I get to hear about it at the store."

"What's going on at the store anyway? I thought the cleaners were done."

"The cleaners are gone," Anna confirmed. "The workmen are finishing up some things today. I am going to open the bookstore tomorrow."

"What about the café?" Cassie asked.

"We need to finish decorating, of course. I am going to round up the girls and pick up the furniture."

"We can order online," Cassie said. "Most big stores have their catalogs on the web now. Join the 21st century, Mom."

"I don't want to use them. I have other ideas."

"Are you going to shop at the thrift store?" Cassie was aghast.

"We picked out a few antique stores. I've also shortlisted some good pieces people are selling."

"Second hand furniture! Can't you do better?"

"I want the café to feel comfortable and cozy. I don't want it to look like those big coffee chains you have in the city."

"Let me know if you want me to go with you," Cassie offered, licking her soup spoon. "This soup gets better every time you make it, Mom."

"It's your Nana's recipe. She let it simmer all day. I don't have that kind of time."

"Does Nana still cook?"

"She doesn't have a big kitchen but I bet that doesn't stop her."

Anna's mother was pushing 80. She lived in a fancy senior home in Southern California near the Mexican border. She had moved there ten years ago after Anna's father died from prostate cancer. To Anna's surprise, her mother had settled in well over there and made a lot of friends. Now they talked once a month and met for Christmas. Her mother had been away on a cruise at John's funeral. Anna had never told her about the cancer, not wanting to worry her. The old woman was mostly oblivious to what was going on in Anna's life.

"Are you going to tell her about Meg?"

Anna had kept Cassie's secret from her mother.

"There's no rush. She won't be here till Christmas."

"All these years, you never mentioned it?"

"What was I going to say? My 16 year old daughter got pregnant and then gave up her child? Nana would have wanted me to raise the baby too."

"How many times are you going to remind me about it, Mom? You think I don't know?"

Anna started clearing the table. Sometimes she wondered if Cassie was really as heartless as she sounded.

"What are you doing tonight?" Cassie asked.

"I forgot all about it. Charlie Robinson sent me some passes for a concert. Some young jazz singer is performing at the Castle Beach Resort."

"Must be the same one I saw the other night," Cassie said. "She's good, Mom. You should go."

"I was going to ask the girls."

"How many passes do you have?"

"It doesn't say. Charlie said it was up to me. I can bring any number of people I want. He had reserved a special table for us."

"They serve champagne during the performance. And the most delicious canapés. It's all very classy."

"I hope it's not too fancy. What am I going to wear?"

"What about that black dress you have with sequins around the neck? Are you taking Gino?"

Anna shook her head.

"You can come with us though, Cassie."

"Awesome! I can use a night out."

"I won't ask Meg, don't worry. I doubt she will be interested in this kind of music."

"Your call, Mom. I didn't say anything."

Anna's head sprang up eagerly as the doorbell rang. She rushed to let Meg in.

"You don't have to use the front door, Meg. Friends and family just walk into the kitchen."

Chapter 13

Anna brushed her hair and observed herself critically in the mirror. The breast conservation surgery she had qualified for had taken a vital chunk off her body. Could people tell her look wasn't entirely natural?

Cassie came in behind her.

"You look great, Mom. Like a million bucks."

"I don't look odd?"

Cassie took her mother by the shoulders and looked into her eyes.

"Listen to me. Back in Hollywood, people pay a big bundle of money to get this kind of work done."

Anna grimaced.

"I didn't ask for this, Cassie."

"Of course you didn't. But it's all worked out very well. Why don't you wear those pearls Dad got you for your 20th anniversary?"

Anna's eyes softened as she pulled out a black box from her jewelry drawer. Cassie could be so likable when she wanted. Anna wondered why her daughter chose to be as prickly as a hedgehog most of the time.

Julie and Mary were also going to the concert with Anna. They were going to meet the Butlers directly at the resort. The full moon hung over the water in a clear sky as Cassie drove up the hill leading to the Castle Beach Resort. It was a beautiful night, Anna thought. She had cheered up after her talk with Cassie and was eagerly looking forward to the evening.

Charlie Robinson stood in the large foyer to welcome them. Dressed in a tuxedo, he looked like he had stepped out from some vintage drama.

"So this is it," Anna said, looking around admiringly. "I think you did a good job here, Charlie."

Charlie Robinson had knocked down a 100 year old door to create a massive and imposing entrance to his hotel. John Butler, head of the local Historic Society had been strongly against it. Charlie and John Butler had fallen out on the issue. Anna decided she wasn't going to let it bother her now.

A young girl dressed in a glittering frock escorted them to the grand ballroom. Julie and Mary were already seated at a table near the stage. The usher pulled out their chairs and offered them champagne. Anna thanked her and accepted a glass of bubbly.

"This is the real deal, Anna," Julie said approvingly. "Drink up."

"What is she doing here?" Cassie hissed, jerking her neck toward the door.

Anna turned around to find the girl from the hotel

escorting Meg into the room. Her face lit up when Meg spotted her and waved. Anna waved back.

"Did you tell her we were coming here?" Anna asked Mary.

Meg was renting a room over Mary's garage.

"I've hardly seen her in the past two days," Mary replied.

Anna saw the girl was ushering Meg to a small table for one set in an alcove. Meg sat down and typed something into her phone. Anna's phone dinged.

"She says her new friend invited her. She had no idea we were coming here."

"Her friend's handing out passes to a fancy concert?" Cassie scoffed.

"Hush, Cassie," Julie warned. "The show's about to begin."

Charlie Robinson stepped on the small stage and welcomed his guests. He gave a brief introduction.

"We are so proud to have the 'Young Ella' staying with us for a while. She has graciously agreed to do a few shows while she's here. Ladies and gentlemen, let me present local California girl and our very own prodigy, Ashley Morton."

There was some polite applause. A young girl dressed in a dazzling red gown came on stage and began singing. Anna found herself mesmerized by her voice. Ashley belted out one hit song after another, captivating the audience. She started off with 'How Deep is the Ocean' by Etta James, went on to Natalie Cole's 'Cry Me a River', then 'My One and Only Love' and 'Summertime' by Ella Fitzgerald.

Anna's eyes glistened with unshed tears and her heart welled up with sweet memories of her husband John. They had both loved these songs, played them on the turntable and danced to them in the candle light when they were first married. Ashley ended her set with 'Dream a Little Dream' and the whole room erupted in applause.

A team of waiters descended on the room, carrying platters loaded with delectable bite sized treats. Charlie Robinson came to their table with the young Ashley on his arm.

"These are my special guests, Ashley." He was staring at Anna with a knowing look in his eyes.

"What a fabulous performance!" Julie exclaimed.

"Brava!" Anna nodded. "You have a gift. My husband and I loved these songs."

"Old is gold," Ashley said sagely. "I love singing them."

"Have we met before?" Anna asked. "You look a bit familiar."

"Are you the lady from that bookstore? I came there a few days ago, remember?"

"Oh yes!"

Ashley waved at someone. Meg walked up to them, looking a bit hesitant.

"You came!" Ashley crowed as she hugged Meg. She took

Meg by the shoulder and pushed her forward. "This is my friend, Meg. She's visiting Dolphin Bay too, just like me."

Anna nodded at Meg but said nothing. She wanted to tell everyone she already knew Meg but that would lead to questions. Cassie hadn't batted an eyelid. She stood there, calmly sipping her champagne.

"You're staying for dinner, aren't you?" Charlie asked Anna. "Mother is so eager to meet you." He nodded at Cassie and the Firecrackers. "You are all invited, of course. Anna's family is always welcome here at Castle Beach."

"We don't want to impose," Cassie murmured.

"I'm already full," Anna said. "I think I had a dozen of these tiny snacks."

"Ashley still has a couple of sets," Charlie said. "It's all arranged."

"You don't want to miss it," Ashley whispered. "Dinner out on the terrace on a full moon night … it's out of this world."

Anna agreed to stay. It would have been rude to decline after such a cordial invite.

"You're staying for dinner too, Meg," Ashley said.

"Any guest of Ashley's is my guest," Charlie added. "See you at dinner, young lady."

The couple walked off to talk to the other guests.

"He's flirting with you, the scamp!" Julie muttered. "What did I tell you?"

Julie wasn't too fond of Charlie Robinson. He had a certain reputation. Rumor had it the Robinson family had been smugglers. Julie was sure Charlie earned his fortune by nefarious means. Anna didn't agree with her. The Robinsons were just a notch above the people in the town, different enough to arouse curiosity and encourage gossip.

Anna took Meg's hands in hers.

"You look pretty, dear. Is this the new friend you were talking about?"

"I had no idea she was such a big deal," Meg said brightly.

Anna watched Cassie glowering at them. She ignored her. A tall man dressed in a suit came over and nudged Cassie. He was accompanied by a pale young woman. Anna realized she was one of the cashiers at the local Paradise Market.

"Dylan! I barely recognized you."

"How are you, Anna?" Dylan smiled. He nodded at Cassie. "Hey Princess!"

"What are you doing here, Dylan?" Cassie's eyes had widened in surprise.

Anna prayed she wouldn't say anything nasty.

"Enjoying an evening of song and dance, just like you."

The band had started playing some music and many

couples had started dancing.

"Have we met?" Dylan asked, looking inquiringly at Meg. "I'm Dylan Woods."

"Dylan is an organic farmer," Anna told Meg. She smiled broadly at Dylan. "This is Meg, my…"

"I work at Bayside Books," Meg interrupted her. "Anna hired me for the summer."

"I've seen you around town," Dylan nodded. "Come over to my farm sometime. It's strawberry season. You can pick as many as you want."

"We'll make a day out of it," Anna said eagerly. "Take a picnic and have lunch on the hill at Daisy Hollow Farms."

"That's a great idea, Anna," Dylan said.

Ashley joined them and put an arm around Meg. She was looking hungrily at Dylan.

"Who's this handsome stranger?"

Anna introduced Dylan again.

"I'm staying here at the resort all this month," Ashley crooned, looking seductively at Dylan. "Do you want to get dinner sometime?"

"Sure," Dylan said. "I'd like that."

He complimented Ashley on her performance.

"Do you write any songs yourself?"

"I do. But I am not allowed to sing them here. Just some stupid contract, you know. My album releases next month and I am going on tour after that. I will be able to sing them at that time."

"Surely you can sing a line or two for us?" Dylan asked.

Ashley simpered and said she might make an exception.

Anna knew how the local women fawned over Dylan. He enjoyed the attention but never crossed a line. Ashley looked like she could take care of herself anyway. Anna wasn't that sure about Meg.

She noticed how Meg hung on to every word Dylan said. From Anna's point of view, it looked like Meg was developing a big crush on him. Was she allowed to remind her granddaughter how old Dylan was?

"Why don't you introduce us to your date, Dylan?" Cassie asked in a silky voice.

Anna didn't know if Cassie was jealous or being protective of her daughter. The ploy worked and the group broke up.

"He's chill," Meg sighed, leaving Anna wondering what she meant.

Chapter 14

Anna looked around her new café proudly.

"The place looks fabulous, Anna," Julie said. "You did a good job."

"We all did," Anna said, arranging her orange thyme cupcakes on a fancy cupcake stand she had bought in a specialty store in San Francisco.

A deep brown couch sat at one end, surrounded with a couple of overstuffed armchairs, a wing chair and a low bench Anna had found at a yard sale. A leather Chesterfield was placed in another corner, with matching chairs and ottomans. There was a rustic table fashioned out of a tree trunk. A few other tables were spread around the space, with comfortable chairs placed around them. It was a space you could relax in for the day, browsing through books and drinking endless cups of coffee.

The large wooden counter had been custom made. A Tiffany lamp rested on it at one end and it was Anna's pride and joy. She planned to fill the space with different kinds of lighting fixtures. And flowers. Fresh flowers!

"Are you planning to name the café?" Mary asked.

"I think it will be Bayside Books for now," Anna said.

"You should call it Anna's and be done with it," Julie

advised. "People coming in directly through the café need some kind of sign on the door."

They discussed other things related to the café, like printing the final menus and sending invitations for the grand opening.

Anna glanced at the clock on the wall and gave her friends a questioning look.

"It's almost noon. Do you think they will come?"

"The ladies never miss a potluck," Mary said. "Of course they will come."

The monthly potluck was a tradition with the local women. Anna had been so busy she had completely forgotten when it was until Julie suggested they have it at the café. It would be a chance to get some early feedback about the ambience.

"I don't know, girls. Lara Crawford's really been on the warpath these past few weeks. Most of the potluck ladies ignore me on the street now."

The bell on the door jingled just then and Sally Davis came in, carrying a slow cooker. She was a teacher at the high school and was a firm believer in Anna's innocence.

"Slow cooker chicken wings as requested."

Mary guided her to a side table they were going to use for the food.

Sally circled the room, exclaiming at everything.

"This place is beautiful, Anna. You did a good job!"

A few more women came in and soon the potluck was in full swing. Anna's cupcakes were tasted and approved by everyone.

"I can't wait for the café to open," a woman said, eating half a cupcake in one bite. "I'll be ordering a dozen of these for Sunday dinner."

Many of the women were also in the Garden Club. They wanted to know if Anna was participating in the upcoming Rose Show.

"I'm planning to," Anna told them.

A couple of hours passed quickly. The Firecrackers collapsed on the leather couch after all the women had left.

"I think that was a success," Julie declared. "You got some free advertising, Anna. These ladies will spread the word about the café."

"Cassie told me about your meeting with Rory," Anna said to Mary. "I didn't get a chance to thank you."

"It was nothing, honey," Mary dismissed. "Rory will do anything for my banana cream pie."

"I don't blame him," Julie laughed. "Why don't we have some more of that pie?"

"We never got a chance to discuss this," Anna said. "I think there may be one more suspect."

She told them about the man who had been following William Parker.

"How are we supposed to track this guy down?" Julie groaned. "Did this Bertha woman tell you anything specific about him?"

Anna shook her head.

"She just described his car. A battered blue sedan with a dent in the passenger door, chipped paint and some kind of colorful sticker on the rear windshield."

"What kind of sticker?" Mary asked.

"Doesn't matter." Julie sat up, her eyes gleaming. "I know that car."

"How?" Anna and Mary chorused.

"I'm almost sure I have seen it parked outside the Yellow Tulip. Not once or twice, several times."

"Let's go there right now," Anna said.

Mary bowed out. "I need to run some errands. I will talk to you gals later."

Anna and Julie walked to the Yellow Tulip diner. Julie began pointing excitedly as soon as they neared the diner's parking lot.

"That's the car I was talking about."

Anna paused to observe the car. It did match Bertha's

description.

"Let's go in," she said eagerly.

They grabbed their usual booth and looked around at the people seated in the diner. It was just after the lunch rush and there were very few people inside. Their usual waitress came over with a pot of coffee.

Anna pointed toward the car in the parking lot.

"Do you know whose car that is?" she asked urgently.

"Sure. Belongs to that gent over there. Sits here all day from breakfast to dinner."

Anna spotted a brown haired man wearing glasses hunched over a computer. He was much younger than her, somewhere in his mid forties if she had to guess.

Julie and Anna got up and went over to this table. Anna cleared her throat and waited for the man to acknowledge them. He looked up after a few seconds.

"Ladies," he nodded, scratching his head. "Can I help you?"

"Are you the owner of that blue sedan outside?" Julie asked.

"Am I blocking you?" the man asked solicitously, pulling out a bunch of keys from his pocket. "Sorry about that."

"The car is fine," Julie said hastily. "We just wanted to ask you something."

"Are you new in town?" Anna asked impulsively. "Haven't seen you around before."

"My name is Joe," the man said, inviting them to sit down. "I'm into sales. I work for an office supplies company headquartered in Idaho. I just got assigned to this region."

"Where is your office?" Anna asked.

"I don't have one," Joe said with a smile. "That's why I work from here. Dolphin Bay is roughly in the centre of my assigned territory. So I've made this diner my HQ. I can be up and on my way whenever I get a call."

"Do you know a man called William Parker?" Anna asked.

"The name doesn't ring a bell," Joe said, scratching his head again. "Why?"

"No reason," Anna said quickly.

She looked at Julie and they stood up.

"Nice talking to you," Anna said.

"You sure my car's not in your way, right?" the man asked Julie.

"He's lying," Julie said as soon as they came out of the diner. "He was a bit too smooth."

"I agree," Anna said. "Now what?"

"Let's go to the police and tell them about this man."

Anna agreed grudgingly. She had no desire to visit the police station.

Teddy Fowler was standing at the front desk when they went inside.

"What are you doing here?" he asked.

Anna told him how Joe had been spotted following William Parker.

"You should question him."

"We don't need advice from civilians. And I don't appreciate you interfering in police business."

"Why don't you get off your high horse and catch the killer then?" Julie snapped.

Anna pulled at her arm and rushed out of the police station.

"Let's go home. I've had enough for one day."

"What about the store?" Julie asked.

"The café's not open yet and Meg's taking care of the bookstore. She can close up."

"Aren't you trusting her too much?"

"You sound like Cassie," Anna grumbled. "Cassie's not sure Meg's who she says she is."

"She's always had trust issues," Julie replied. "But I think she's right this time."

Julie drove them to Anna's house. Anna started a pot of coffee as soon as she went in.

"I'm going to call Gino," she said. "He will give us the right advice."

Gino urged Anna not to lose her cool and promised to call back soon.

The two friends sat sipping their coffee, too tired to argue or discuss anything. Cassie came out of her room, followed by a tall, buff man with a chiseled face.

"Bobby's here," she said.

Anna's eyes widened when she laid eyes on Cassie's friend. So she had called in the troops. Maybe Bobby would talk some sense into her daughter.

"It's nice to finally meet you, Bobby."

"I put him in the guest room," Cassie told her. "We are going out for a drive."

"Is that the guy she talks to all the time?" Julie asked as soon as they left.

"Bobby's the only one she opens up to," Anna nodded. "I'm glad he's here for her."

The phone rang and Gino's face flashed on the screen.

Anna grabbed the phone and listened to what he had to say.

"That's good to know, Gino, but I can't leave it up to them. Not while I'm still in the hot seat."

Gino agreed with her, warned her to be careful and hung up.

"The police are looking at other suspects," she told Julie after she hung up. "But that's not good enough for me."

"I agree. So what's the next step?"

Anna admitted she was clueless.

"I need to clear my head."

"You're making pasta, aren't you?"

Chapter 15

Cassie came home with Bobby to find the table in the dining room set for a formal meal. The house smelled of roasted garlic and something equally delicious. Cassie was pleased to know Anna had made an effort. Bobby was her bestie and he was visiting them for the first time. She wanted him to feel special.

She stole a glance at Bobby. He was looking his usual cool self. Cassie had taken him to the Coastal Walk and then to her favorite vantage point to watch the sunset. As the sun went down over the water, she had told him everything about Meg. Bobby was the only person Cassie had ever confided in about her teen folly so he already knew Cassie was a mother. But Meg's arrival surprised him too.

"Does she look like you?" he asked. "Is she shy? Have you talked to her?"

"Hold on a second, Bobbykins. You are sounding just like my mother. I don't know if I even want to believe this girl."

"Why not?"

"Well, she just turned up out of nowhere. What do we really know about her?"

"You think she's an impostor?" Bobby asked.

Cassie gave a shrug. She felt like a heel saying it, but she needed to speak her mind. That's what Bobby was there for.

"I don't know what to think, Bobby. This has completely knocked me down."

"Your mother kept your secret all these years, right?" Bobby asked her. "And you're the only one who knew about the baby."

"The Firecrackers knew," Cassie reminded him, explaining who they were. "And the nuns at the place where I gave birth."

"They are not going to give you away. Why would they, after all these years?"

"My mother actually posted something on an online forum. Meg read that and came looking for us. That's what makes it seem fishy to me."

Bobby placed an arm around Cassie and took her hand in his.

"I don't like saying this, babe, but I think you don't want to face the truth."

Cassie wondered if that was true.

"You have thought about her all these years, haven't you?" Bobby asked, the only person privy to Cassie's innermost thoughts. "This is a gift. This is your chance to get to know her, build a relationship with her."

"That's what Mom says."

"I think Anna is a wise woman."

"I haven't been very welcoming to Meg," Cassie admitted. "Not that I was rude …"

"You can take your time," Bobby said softly. "You will need it. I know it's not a switch you can just turn on."

"I'm still going ahead with the background check."

"That makes sense," Bobby agreed with her. "Even if it sounds a bit callous, it's the smart thing to do. And I think you should do the blood test too."

"Meg might not agree."

"I think she will," Bobby said thoughtfully. "So, when do I meet this kid of yours?"

"Mom gave her a job at the store. I'll take you there tomorrow before you leave."

"What about the paparazzi?" Bobby asked. "Are you sending out a press release?"

"I haven't thought that far. We will need to introduce her to people in the town at some point."

Bobby advised Cassie to do it soon. Cassie thanked him for coming all the way to Dolphin Bay to let her cry on his shoulder.

"You're the best, Bobby. What would I do without you?"

"I'm here for you, always."

Cassie was in a better mood as they walked home.

Anna came out of her room, wearing a fresh coat of lipstick and a new dress.

"You're back!" she exclaimed. "Just in time for dinner."

Meg walked in through the kitchen, looking a bit hesitant. Cassie frowned when she saw her.

"Anna told me to use the kitchen door," Meg spluttered. "I hope that's fine."

"Of course it is," Anna stepped in. "Come, come. Meet Cassie's friend."

Cassie placed a hand on Bobby's shoulder.

"This is Bobby," she told Meg. "He lives in Los Angeles."

"Is he your bae?"

"That's right, sweetie," Bobby said, offering his hand to Meg.

Anna was looking bewildered.

"She means is he my best friend?" Cassie explained.

"Oh." Anna's face cleared. "Bobby means a lot to Cassie. He's seen her through a lot of rough times."

"Is that why you're here?" Meg asked frankly.

Cassie gave Bobby a warning look.

"I've missed Cassie since she came here. My schedule opened up for a day so I decided to come visit."

Cassie hoped that answer was good enough for Meg. She wasn't getting any other explanation.

"I could use a glass of wine," Bobby said. "I'm feeling parched after all that walking."

"I thought you only drank that green stuff," Anna teased. "Are you sure a glass of wine won't upset your calorie quota for the day?"

"Ha, Ha. Good one, Anna."

"When can we eat, Mom?" Cassie asked, pulling up a chair at the table.

She lifted the lid off a few pots.

"You made tortellini!"

Meg helped Anna serve the salad. There was balsamic grilled chicken topped with basil pesto and mushroom tortellini with green peas and mint and a creamy porcini and white wine sauce.

Bobby couldn't stop raving about the food.

"What did you do all day?" Anna asked Cassie.

"I almost forgot," Cassie said, taking a sip of her wine. "I went to meet that EMT."

Meg and Bobby were brought up to speed on the

bookstore incident and Anna's predicament. They already knew some of it.

"Did Bobby go with you, Cassie?"

"This was before he got here," Cassie explained. "I was getting bored sitting around here so I thought I would go visit this guy."

"I'm surprised he entertained you," Anna said.

"He was quite open about it," Cassie said. "He made it clear how much he hated William Parker. But he still loves his wife and they are making a go of it."

"What about the child?"

"Ethan is raising it as his own. The child doesn't know all this, of course. He's too young."

"So they are a happy family," Anna observed.

"As far as I could tell," Cassie nodded. "And he has an alibi. The family was on a camping trip in Yosemite for the whole week. One of the neighbors confirmed it. Ethan's got one of those Airstream trailers, it seems. They loaded it up and left a few days before William Parker died and didn't get back until a few days after."

"So Ethan has a strong motive but no opportunity," Meg spoke up.

"Did you say this guy was poisoned?" Bobby asked, taking a second helping of the pasta. He complimented Anna on the food again. "No wonder Cassie's putting on the pounds," he teased. "She's eating like this and missing her workouts."

"I barely gained ten pounds, Bobbykins," Cassie protested. "I can lose it in a month."

"It's boot camp for you once you get back home," Bobby promised.

"Do you still think of Hollywood as your home?" Meg asked Cassie.

Cassie answered her by taking a big gulp of wine.

"Anyway," Bobby said. "What I was going to say is, poison is supposed to be a woman's weapon, right?"

"That's the funny thing," Anna replied. "We haven't come across a woman yet. There's Ethan, of course. We just ruled him out. William Parker had a fight with his business partner. We haven't met him yet. Then there is another guy who seems suspicious but no woman."

"What about Ethan's wife, Mom?" Cassie asked. "Do you think she might have done it?"

"Wasn't she on that camping trip too?" Meg asked.

"Oh yeah, right," Cassie nodded.

"I keep coming back to the same question," Anna said. "How or why did he end up at my bookstore?"

Cassie wondered if she was partially to blame. She didn't remember if she had locked the bookstore that night before heading to the concert. Now it looked like someone had taken advantage of the open door. Why hadn't Anna said anything about it to her? Cassie realized her mother was being protective.

"What's for dessert?" Bobby asked. "Cassie can't stop raving about your tiramisu."

"I made a pan," Anna smiled. "And there's gelato if anyone wants it."

"Do you like dessert, Meg?" Cassie asked. "What's your favorite?"

"My Mom makes the best apple pie," Meg replied. "But I'm beginning to like Anna's tiramisu."

Cassie stole a glance at Bobby. He smiled approvingly. She had made an effort to be nice and it hadn't been too hard. Cassie reminded herself to call Gino in the morning. Once he confirmed Meg's identity, she would get the blood test done. Then she could finally begin to bond with her daughter.

Cassie watched Anna serve big slices of tiramisu on the dessert plates. Meg took a big bite and rubbed her stomach, just like Cassie used to do when she was a child.

Chapter 16

Anna was feeling upbeat the next morning. The dinner with Bobby had gone better than she expected. Cassie had behaved herself. Meg had been polite as usual. Anna had sensed a thaw in Cassie's demeanor and wondered if she had Bobby to thank for it.

Cassie had left early to drop Bobby off at the airport in San Francisco. Planning to open the bookstore at 9 AM, Anna rushed through her coffee and breakfast. It had been a while since she spent time at the store and she was looking forward to it. She made avocado toast and set some aside for Cassie. She debated taking some of it to the store for Meg, then decided against it. Mary would make sure Meg had a hearty breakfast.

Meg was standing on the sidewalk under the magnolia tree when Anna cycled up. The pink and white blossoms scented the air with their lemony fragrance.

"You are here early."

"It's a minute past 9. I try to be punctual."

Anna unlocked the door and went in with Meg. She went into the small pantry and started a pot of coffee.

"I always put the coffee on when I come in," she told Meg. "I guess that will change once the café is up and running."

"Do you have any chores for me?" Meg asked. "There's not much to do. I have just been sitting behind the desk for the past couple of days."

"I dust the shelves when I come in and tidy up. Set the newspapers out on that reading table over there. Then I tidy up every few hours. That's pretty much it, other than ringing up people who make purchases."

"That sounds easy. I think I can do all this and help you at the café."

"We'll see," Anna said, fixing their coffee. "Do you take cream or sugar?"

"Lots of cream and four sugars, please."

"I'm going next door for a while," Anna said after she finished her coffee. "Will you be alright here?"

"Don't worry about me, Anna. This is not my first job."

Anna reminded herself to ask Meg about that sometime.

She went out and stood on the sidewalk, staring up at the sign on the store next to hers. Records Old and New had been there much before she opened Bayside Books. The owner Otto was an eccentric old man who hated Anna. It had started when Anna began to stock music CDs in her store. Otto felt she was encroaching on his territory. Anna argued that wasn't true because he only sold vinyl. John had suggested a truce. Anna agreed not to sell any music in her store. Otto never forgave her though. He barely said hello to her when they ran into each other on the street.

"What are you doing here?" Otto growled when Anna entered his store.

Shoulder length hair, a flowing beard and moon shaped glasses sat on a tanned face with leathery skin. Otto was a diehard surfer who liked to ride the waves in his spare time.

"I'm good, thanks, Otto."

"People are talking about you."

"About that ... were you here that night, Otto? Did you see anything suspicious?"

Otto wanted to know what day she was talking about. Anna told him the exact date.

"I closed up early that night but I guess I can check the security footage."

"You have a camera?" Anna's eyes popped out. "Why didn't you say anything all this time?"

"No one asked me." Otto shrugged. "You want to see it or not? I haven't got all day."

Anna followed Otto to the back of the store. There was a tiny office with a computer. Otto flipped through some folders and located one with the date Anna had given. The video began to play.

"It's too dark," Anna muttered.

A pair of lights appeared on the screen and a van pulled up in front of the door. Anna held her breath as the door started to slide open. The screen went blank for a second and the video started playing again.

"What just happened?"

"Dunno," Otto grumbled.

"Can you play it again, please?"

Otto played the video again twice. It cut off at the same point every time. Anna slammed her fist on the desk in frustration.

"Hey, watch it, sister."

"Are you sure you don't have any other tapes of the day?"

"This is not a tape. The camera uploads the video in some cloud and generates a file for each day. Looks like something went wrong that day."

"Why am I not surprised?" Anna muttered.

"Are we done here?"

Anna forced herself to control her emotions.

"Let's just see if we can see that van clearly, maybe read the plates or something."

Anna took some pictures of the screen with her phone. There was something painted on the side but it wasn't clearly visible.

"Looks like some kind of contractors," Otto said, pointing

to a small word on the screen.

"You can read that?" Anna asked, squinting her eyes.

"Got 20-20 vision. Wanted to be a pilot but didn't have enough dough to take lessons."

Anna had never known that little tidbit about Otto. She thanked him for his help and walked out in a daze, staring at her phone screen.

"What are you looking at?" Meg asked when Anna walked into Bayside Books.

Anna told her what she had found. Meg took the phone from her and did some weird things with her fingers.

"I'm trying to magnify the image," she told Anna. "This says 'r and Sons' on the top line. The line below that says 'fing Contractors'. A lot of the text is cut off, Anna."

"Fing Contractors? Roofing Contractors!" Anna cried. "I know what that first line must be. Buckner and Sons."

Meg was looking at her in wonder.

"How did you figure that out, Anna?"

"Tim Buckner was William Parker's partner. They had a falling out. He has his own business in Blackberry Beach now."

"Is he one of the suspects on your list?"

Anna nodded. "I need to go talk to him now."

"Don't go alone," Meg said quickly. "Call Mary or Julie or check if Cassie's back."

"Cassie won't be back yet," Anna said, shaking her head. "I know! Let me call Gino."

Gino promised to get there in half an hour. Anna waited for him at the corner of the street at the given time. Soon she was bringing him up to speed on what she had done that morning.

"That was brilliant, Anna. How did you connect the dots so soon?"

"Tim Buckner has been on my list of suspects," Anna replied. "Julie and I were supposed to go and see him but that never happened."

They reached the town of Blackberry Beach half an hour later and Gino followed the navigation system to the address. Buckner and Sons was a small unit in a strip mall with a large freshly painted sign hanging over their store.

A burly man with a red Mohawk and matching red sideburns that covered half his cheeks looked up when they entered. His piercing green eyes bore into Anna's, making her shiver. A younger version of the man sat at an adjoining desk, sporting a matching red Mohawk. Anna decided neither color came from a bottle.

"What can I do for you?"

"Are you are the same Tim Buckner who used to work with William Parker?"

"Who's asking?"

Gino took a step forward and introduced himself.

"I know who you are. I lived in Dolphin Bay all my life. Still live there, in fact. Only reason we had to open a business here is because of that blackguard."

"But now that William Parker is dead, you can set up shop in Dolphin Bay," Anna summed up.

"What are you trying to say?" Tim growled.

"What were you doing on the night Parker was killed?" Gino asked.

"You don't have to tell him nothing, Dad." The young Mohawk spoke up.

"If you know who I am, you know I still got contacts in the force," Gino warned. "You can either come clean now or go to the police station."

"Alright, alright, what do you want?"

"You have a dark colored van, right?" Anna asked. "What was it doing in front of my store on the night of the murder?"

"Van was stolen," Tim sighed. "Found it a block away from the corner of Ocean and Main a couple of days later."

"That's where my store is!" Anna exclaimed. "On the corner of Ocean and Main."

"Where was it stolen from?" Gino asked sternly.

"Right where we always park it," Tim replied. "In the lot behind the Yellow Tulip near that dumpster. It's got all our ladders and stuff, see?"

He gave a lengthy explanation of how it was convenient to keep the van in a central place and drive it to work sites from there rather than take it home every time.

"Where were you when the car was stolen?" Gino wanted to know.

"I was at that fancy resort up on the hill," Tim said sullenly.

Anna realized they weren't going to get much more out of Tim. She nodded at Gino and they went out.

"Do you trust him?" Anna asked as Gino drove them home.

"I don't know, Anna. We need to check his alibi first. I'm also going to talk to Teddy Fowler about this."

"He didn't seem like a blues fan to me. What do you think he was doing at the resort?"

Gino burst out laughing.

"You never know, Anna."

"We are nowhere close to solving this, are we?" Anna asked, her brow settling in a frown.

Chapter 17

Cassie drove to the airport with Bobby, letting him talk.

"This might be a good thing for your career. You are not getting any lead roles. Having a young daughter might make you a candidate for those mother type roles."

"What? I may be getting old for playing a 20 something. But I'm not playing anyone's mother."

"Just sayin'," Bobby shrugged.

They were both quiet for a while.

"Meg seems like a good kid. And she's fully grown."

"What does that have to do with anything?" Cassie grumbled. "You sound like my mother, Bobby. Infatuated with Meg."

Cassie pulled up in the departure zone of the airport and Bobby jumped out. He grabbed his bag from the back seat and blew Cassie a kiss.

"Keep your cool, babe. Talk soon."

Cassie pulled out before the traffic cop standing on the pavement could yell at her to move. She had a long drive ahead of her and a lot on her mind. She dialed Gino from the car. She wanted to know if he had made any progress on her request. She got his voicemail and hung up without leaving a message. Anna was meeting her at the Tipsy Whale for lunch. Cassie expected she would bring Meg along.

Anna was sitting at a window booth inside the pub, alone. She raised a hand when she saw Cassie.

"Where's Meg?"

"She's at the store, working. I can bring her a sandwich when we leave."

"What have you been up to, Mom?" Cassie asked. "Have you talked to Gino lately?"

"I just met him."

Anna told Cassie about going to meet Tim Buckner.

"Do you remember seeing him at the resort? Tall, burly guy with bright red hair? Kind of hard to miss."

"I don't remember. But that doesn't mean anything. You heard Ashley sing. I was completely engrossed in her performance. Then there was Teddy and his wife. I wasn't exactly checking out the other guests."

"Tim Buckner says he's lived in town all his life. But I don't remember coming across him."

"Clearly, you don't move in the same circles, Mom."

"There have to be people in town who know about him. I wonder if Murphy will know."

She glanced at the pub owner laughing heartily with some guests.

"He has a small business, right?" Cassie mused. "And he places ads in the Yellow Pages or the newspaper? What about someone at the Chronicle?"

"That's a brilliant idea, Cassie. You know who's the editor of the Chronicle? Ian Samuels, your old English teacher."

"Mr. Samuels from high school?" Cassie laughed. "Really? I'd forgotten about him."

"Why don't you go revive your acquaintance?" Anna asked with a gleam in her eyes. "I hear he loves to gossip."

"Soon as we finish lunch," Cassie promised.

They ordered the special as usual. It was a fried fish sandwich made with beer battered cod sprinkled with vinegar and a creamy dill sauce. Cassie swooned over the sweet potato fries it was served with.

"I'm heading back to the store," Anna said after they sat back with a satisfied smile on their faces. "Do you want me to show you where the Chronicle is?"

"I can find it, Mom." Cassie pulled up a map on her phone.

"Give my regards to Ian," Anna said as they walked out of the Tipsy Whale.

Cassie didn't have far to go. The Dolphin Bay Chronicle offices were situated a couple of blocks off Main Street. Cassie decided to work off her lunch and started walking.

A short, plump man with a shiny bald head and grey hair growing out of his ears cried in delight when Cassie walked into his office.

"Is that you, Cassie Butler?" He took off his glasses and peered at her.

"Mr. Samuels!" Cassie gave him a hug. "What are you doing here?"

"The Chronicle was floundering after the old editor died. They offered me this position. Retirement wasn't going too well for me. I was just bored, you know. So I took up this job."

Mr. Samuels told her how he had watched every movie she had been in several times.

"You got me started, Mr. Samuels," Cassie reminisced. "Remember that production of Romeo and Juliet in middle school?"

"You were the best Juliet I ever came across as a drama coach," Ian Samuels said. "You were barely 14 at that time. Always knew you would make me proud."

Ian rang for coffee and finally turned to business.

"What brings you here, child?"

"A man was found dead in my mother's bookstore."

"I know about William Parker. The Chronicle reported it, of course."

"The police suspect Mom so ..."

"Anna? She'd never hurt a fly."

Cassie wondered how Ian Samuels hadn't heard the rumors the mayor was spreading about her mother. Maybe he was just being polite.

"Mom's trying to figure out what might have happened. I'm helping her."

"Your mother's a smart cookie. Didn't she find out what happened to that poor college girl?"

Cassie nodded.

"We came across someone called Tim Buckner. It seems he used to be the dead guy's partner. Have you ever heard of him?"

"Have I? William Parker and Tim Buckner were partners for years. They had a good thing going with clients in and around Dolphin Bay. Tim was grooming his son to take over when he retired. Then something went wrong."

"What happened?"

"Some money was found missing from their company. William was accused of embezzlement. He pointed the finger at Tim. Tim maintained he was innocent. There was a big scandal."

"When did this happen?" Cassie asked.

"A couple of years ago as far as I remember. Tim finally got out of the business. He and his son started their own gig in Blackberry Beach."

"Did he go quietly?"

"Tim Buckner is many things but he's not quiet. He has a mean temper, Cassie. Rumor is he made all kinds of threats against William when he left."

"So would you say he had a motive?"

Ian's look said it all.

"Why wait two years to kill him though?"

"Maybe he was waiting for the right chance?" Ian quizzed. "Thanks for bringing this to me, Cassie. I had forgotten all about Tim Buckner."

"Do you really believe he's guilty?"

"I believe he's capable. I might spin that into a story."

"It was great catching up with you, Mr. Samuels. Did you know Mom is opening a café in town? You should come to the grand opening. Consider this an official invitation."

"Anna's café is the talk of the town. We will do a story on it once it's up and running."

Cassie got up to leave.

"Here's a thought, Cassie. William Parker's lawyer should have details about this feud between him and Tim. Why don't you go see him? He might know if anyone else had a problem with William. He wasn't very well liked, to be honest."

"That's a great idea, Mr. Samuels."

Cassie thanked him and walked out of the Chronicle, happy she had some new information for Anna. She debated going to the bookstore. The thought of running into Meg held her back.

Cassie walked to the parking lot and got into her car. The beat up old Mercedes started after half a dozen tries. Cassie decided to go for a drive. A few minutes later, she realized where she was when a sign for Daisy Hollow Farms appeared on her left. On an impulse, she swung onto a dirt road.

Daisy Hollow Farms was a bustling operation, much larger and organized than what she remembered. She had come there twenty years ago on one fateful rainy afternoon. Had she been wrong to break up with Dylan all those years ago? But she was just a hurt and confused teenager. What did she know?

The object of her reverie stepped out of a barn, dressed in faded overalls. He waved at her and walked over, a wide grin on his face.

"Hello Princess! Lost your way?"

"I was in the area and I thought I might see what the fuss is about. Mom goes on and on about how fancy this place is now."

"Nothing fancy as you can see," Dylan said, waving an arm

around. "Just working the land like my ancestors did." He sobered as he looked at Cassie. "It's a far cry from Hollywood."

"So does one get a tour?" Cassie asked, stepping out of the car.

Dylan gave an exaggerated bow and offered her his arm. Cassie ignored him and started walking toward a field planted with strawberries. A bushel of strawberries lay in the path. Cassie took a couple of the juicy, red fruits and popped one in her mouth. She closed her eyes to savor the sweet flavor.

Dylan showed her where they processed the milk and made cheese. A woman came over with a brown paper bag bursting with strawberries.

"Take these to Anna," Dylan said.

Cassie started to open her bag to pay him.

"On the house, Princess!"

"Do you have to call me that?" Cassie fumed.

"There was a time when you liked it," Dylan said, lowering his voice to a whisper.

"Times change, Dylan," Cassie snapped.

"You know that new girl who's working for Anna?" Dylan asked casually as he walked her back to her car.

Cassie tried to hide the sudden shiver that ran through her.

"She reminds me of you."

Chapter 18

Anna lifted the lid off the pan and breathed in the heady aroma of herbs and spices. She hoped Gino liked Thai food.

Cassie came in, looking tired but pleased with herself.

"Something smells awesome, Mom."

"Dinner in half an hour. If you want to take a shower, now's the time."

Cassie nodded and hurried into her room.

Anna began setting the table, wondering what Meg was doing that evening. She had hesitated over inviting her along with Gino but Meg had made it easy for her, saying she wanted to make some phone calls back home. Maybe she missed her parents. Anna hoped she would get an opportunity to thank them sometime for taking such good care of Meg.

The doorbell rang and Anna scrambled to check herself in the hall mirror before answering the door. Gino stood outside, holding a bunch of daisies in his hand. He handed them to Anna.

"These are lovely, Gino. Thanks so much."

"How are you, Anna?" Gino asked, following her into the

kitchen.

"I'm doing fine," Anna assured him. "Didn't we meet just a few hours ago?"

"Feels much longer than that," Gino murmured in her ear, making her blush.

Cassie joined them, greeting Gino with a knowing smile on her face.

"What have you cooked, Anna. Smells like lemongrass."

"I'm impressed," Anna replied. "I made red curry salmon poached in coconut milk. There's pineapple fried rice to go with it."

"Sounds delicious," Gino said, patting his stomach. "Let's eat already."

"Did you meet Ian Samuels?" Anna asked Cassie as they began eating.

"Meeting Mr. Samuels was a really great idea, Mom."

She told them about her conversation with the Chronicle editor.

"We need to find out more about this lawyer he mentioned and go talk to him."

"He must have used one of the lawyers in town," Anna mused. "Maybe Tim Buckner will tell us who this lawyer is."

"You think so?" Cassie asked. "Why would he help us?"

"If he's innocent, he will be eager to get a clean chit. Especially if he wants to start doing business in Dolphin Bay again."

They all took second helpings of the salmon. Anna was secretly glad she had made extra.

"This pineapple fried rice hits the spot, Anna," Gino praised. "It goes really well with that hot curry sauce."

"I took a cooking class when we were in Thailand."

"You're quite the traveler, aren't you?" Gino said in wonder. "I knew you had been to Europe, but all the way to Thailand? That's something."

"Cassie was shooting one of her films over there," Anna explained. "She sent us tickets. It was a wonderful trip. So anyway, a local woman was offering cooking classes in Chiang Mai. John loved spicy food so he urged me to take this class."

"You still miss him, don't you?" Gino asked.

Anna nodded.

"I don't think I will ever stop loving him."

"Of course you won't," Gino said gently. "I think you are more fortunate than most, to have found this kind of love in your lifetime."

Anna stood up to get dessert. It was coconut ice cream

with mango syrup and chopped hazelnuts.

"Thanks for a tasty dinner, Anna," Gino said, sitting back in his chair. "Now can we talk business?"

"You have some news." Anna took a deep breath. "Good or bad?"

"Both, actually," Gino sighed. "I spoke with my contacts. The police have almost cleared you, Anna. So you are off the hook."

Cassie cheered. "Isn't that good news?"

"I'm afraid that's not all, Cassie. You ladies are still tied in."

"What does that mean?" Anna asked fearfully.

"Cassie's on the radar now," Gino said.

"But why?" Anna and Cassie cried out together.

"What have I done?" Cassie asked, dismayed. "I didn't know William Parker."

"No," Gino agreed. "But your Mom did."

Anna was struck dumb by what Gino said next.

"You will never believe what the police found during their investigation. It seems William Parker was at the Castle Beach Resort that night, attending the same concert Cassie did."

"Why would he go there?" Anna asked.

"He must have bought a ticket," Gino shrugged. "Maybe he was a blues fan. This gives Cassie an opportunity to have poisoned him."

"Will anyone believe I didn't know this guy?" Cassie cried. "Why would I poison him?"

"For Anna," Gino replied. "Lara Crawford is sure he saw something that will incriminate your mother in your father's death. Anna wanted to silence him. You, being her loyal daughter, offered to do it for her."

"That's fantastic!" Anna snapped. "Even more fantastic than their previous theory."

"This is how the police work," Gino said. "They come up with a theory and try to prove it."

"But I'm innocent," Cassie objected. "You believe that, don't you?"

"One thing's clear," Anna said grimly. "We can't give up just yet. I'm going to continue doing what I was." She turned to Gino. "I am sure that man at the diner wasn't telling us the truth. Will you come with me? He might sing a different tune when you talk to him."

"I don't mind," Gino said. "Tell me when you want to go."

Anna's head began pounding. She began rubbing her forehead with her fingers while Gino and Cassie cleared the table. She could barely follow their conversation while they loaded the dishwasher and made small talk about upcoming events at Gino's winery.

"What's the matter, Mom?" Cassie asked with concern as she wiped her hands with a dish towel.

Gino's face clouded.

"Don't worry, Anna. You'll be fine."

"I feel a bit lightheaded," Anna finally admitted.

"Of course you do!" Cassie exclaimed. "You've been running around all day. How long were you slaving over that stove, Mom? You gotta take it easy."

"Don't fuss, Cassie."

"I won't listen this time," Cassie said. "Let's go sit in the living room. You are putting your feet up for a while."

Anna let Cassie take her arm. They went into the living room. She thought Gino would leave but he sat down in a chair opposite her.

"I'm going to stick around, just in case," he said.

Anna saw the concern in his eyes and felt touched.

"Why don't you tell us about your special rose, Mom?" Cassie said, pulling out a bottle of brandy from a cabinet.

She poured the brandy in small glasses and handed one to Gino and Anna.

"This is your father's cognac," Anna mumbled. "It's almost gone."

"We'll get a new bottle," Cassie said. "Now tell us about this rose."

Anna sat back and closed her eyes. She started speaking after a minute.

"Your father had the green thumb in the family. You know I'm practically useless in the garden."

Anna took a sip of her brandy and savored the warmth as it trickled down her throat.

"John wanted to create a special rose. It was going to be cream, edged with dark red with a heady fragrance and the most velvety petals. He named it Eloise after his mother. John worked on this rose for many years until it was exactly like he wanted."

"Do we have this rose in our garden now?" Cassie asked.

"We do," Anna nodded. "The gardener takes care of it."

"Why don't you enter this in the Rose Show?" Gino asked.

"I want to," Anna said. "I've lost track of whether they are still accepting entries. I will have to ask Mary about it."

"Can I get you anything else?" Cassie asked solicitously.

Anna assured Cassie she was alright.

"It's getting late," she said. "I think I'm going to turn in now." She looked at Gino. "You are free to stay as long as you want. But be warned, Cassie might rope you into watching Casablanca."

Gino threw back his head and laughed.

"Honestly, I wouldn't mind that. But there's just one more thing I wanted to discuss before you go, Anna. It won't take long."

Anna tensed. "What is it?"

"It's about Meg. You know Cassie asked me to look into her background."

"What did you find?" Cassie burst out.

"Nothing much," Gino told them. "I had someone run a background check. She's clean, as far as I can tell. I see an address for her in Muncie, Indiana. She's only twenty so if she had any kind of record as a minor, it's sealed now."

"She's from the Midwest," Anna conceded. "I think she must have moved around the state quite a bit."

"But do you think she's telling the truth?" Cassie asked Gino.

"Only one way to be sure, Cassie," Gino sighed. "Are you ready for that test?"

Chapter 19

Anna rushed through her routine the next morning. Gino was going to pick her up and they were going to get breakfast at the Yellow Tulip diner.

Cassie walked into the kitchen, rubbing her eyes.

"You look all dressed up."

"No, I'm not! And Good Morning to you too."

"Oh yeah, you're meeting Gino, aren't you? Are those earrings new?"

"Meg and I got them in San Francisco."

Cassie rolled her eyes at that.

"I guess I'm eating cereal for breakfast."

"Will you go open the bookstore at 9? Meg will be there all day so you can come back whenever you want."

"Why don't you get a pair of keys made for Meg?"

Anna missed the sarcasm. "I'm going to do just that."

Gino arrived soon and helped Anna into his truck. He parked at the edge of Main Street and they walked to the Yellow Tulip.

"About last night … I'm a bit concerned, Anna. Does Cassie really think you are in any danger from Meg?"

"Cassie has fanciful ideas. It's the Hollywood influence."

"Her concern for you is genuine. If she has any doubts, I would pay close attention to them."

"Duly noted," Anna said. "Now let's go in and get a greasy, unhealthy breakfast. What do they call it? Breakfast of the champions?"

"I'm right behind you," Gino said, rubbing his hands.

They found an empty booth and sat down. Anna looked around, trying to spot the man they were after.

"He's not here yet."

"He can wait," Gino said. "Let's eat first."

They ordered the breakfast special, a large platter with sausage patties, bacon, eggs and two pancakes. Anna chose the blueberry pancakes and Gino went for chocolate chip.

"Do you really think Cassie's in trouble?" Anna asked Gino as she poured hot sauce over her eggs.

"They will call her in for questioning at the very least."

"Why is this happening to me, Gino? I've lead a blameless life. Been a model citizen of this town. Why me?"

"I can't answer that, Anna," Gino said gravely. "But whatever happens, I will be in your corner. I can promise you that."

They took their time enjoying the food. The waitress came and topped up their coffee. She gave Anna a knowing look. Anna figured there would be some fresh gossip about her and Gino spreading through town pretty soon.

Anna had just finished her second cup of coffee when she spotted their target. She sat up suddenly.

"He's here," she said under her breath.

"Relax," Gino cautioned. "We don't want to spook him."

Anna drummed her fingers on the table nervously, waiting until their quarry found a booth and ordered something. She waited for a nod from Gino before walking over to the man.

"Hello." Gino announced his presence. "I'm Gino Mancini. Can we talk?"

The man nodded and closed his laptop.

"What can I do for you?"

If he recognized Anna from their earlier meeting, he didn't show it.

"You implied you barely knew William Parker but I know that's not true. You were seen following him. And you had some kind of altercation outside his house. I have proof."

She finally stopped to catch her breath.

"Why don't you sit down?" the man asked, pointing to the empty seat before him.

"And I don't buy that stuff about you being some kind of salesman," Anna burst out.

"You're right," the man finally admitted. He offered his hand to Gino. "I'm Joey Bellinger. I'm a journalist for a national publication."

"What are you doing in Dolphin Bay?" Gino asked. "Chasing a story?"

"You can say that," Joey nodded. "But I'm afraid I can't tell you more than that at this time."

"What was your connection to William Parker? Was he part of your story?"

"Like I said, I can't comment on that."

"You don't need to," Anna snorted. "We can put two and two together."

"Can you tell us why you were arguing with Parker?" Gino asked.

Joey pursed his mouth and glanced out of the window. He seemed to come to a decision.

"William Parker had a cabin in the woods. He spent a lot of time there. It was like a secret hideout. I was asking him about it when he flared up and started lashing out."

"What's this cabin got to do with anything?" Anna asked.

"And so he went to this cabin. Why should that bother you?"

"I can't talk about that," Joey said.

Anna opened her mouth to protest but Gino put a warning hand on her back.

"Thanks for talking to us, Joey," she said instead and walked out. "That wasn't very helpful, was it?" she asked Gino. "Journalist! How do we know he's not lying again?"

"I'm going to check his credentials," Gino told her. "But I think he was telling the truth this time. Most investigative journalists are very careful when they are working on a story. So I'm not surprised he doesn't want to talk."

"What about that cabin?" Anna asked.

"I think I might know that place he mentioned. Let me check a few things, Anna."

They walked toward the parking lot, passing by Anna's bookstore. Anna peeped in and saw Meg ringing up a customer.

"Well, well, well!" A familiar voice rang out, making Anna whirl.

"If it isn't the famous husband killer."

"Be very careful what you say, Lara," Gino warned. "You can't go around slandering people."

Lara Crawford, the mayor of Dolphin Bay, ignored him and

trained her eyes on Anna.

"You're going away for a double murder, Anna. Get your things in order."

"Don't you have anything better to do?" Anna asked her. "Like doing something good for the town for a change?"

Lara's mouth twisted in a grimace.

"I'm pulling you off the streets, aren't I?"

"Leave her alone, Lara," Gino said, taking Anna's hand.

He gently turned her around and started walking to his truck. Anna sighed when she climbed in.

"You know what bothers me most about Lara? I don't know what she has against me. Why is she doing this? We were never good friends but she was at least civil."

"Hard to say what motivates someone," Gino said. "Just ignore her. If she gets too pesky, call your lawyer and ask him to sue her for defamation."

"Surely it won't come to that?"

"It's your call, Anna."

Gino asked Anna what her plans were for the rest of the day.

"Meg's taking care of the store so I don't have to rush anywhere. What do you have in mind?"

Gino told her to wait and made a couple of calls.

"Hang on," he said, easing the truck into drive. "We are going to meet an old friend of mine."

Gino drove to the Sunshine Acres Senior Center. A cheerful nurse greeted them with a wide smile and walked them to a lounge.

"He's playing chess with one of his cronies. I'll bring him to you."

She came back with a stooping old man who was pushing a walker. He had a full head of snow white hair and sharp blue eyes. He seemed to brighten when he saw Gino.

"How are you, boy? So you finally found time for me."

Gino introduced Anna as his friend. An aide came by and offered them coffee.

"I rarely get visitors," the old man said. "They must be wondering who you are. I'm going to dine on this for days."

"Dan here is my father's friend," Gino told Anna. "He used to be around when I grew up."

He turned to Dan as he sipped his coffee.

"What happened to that cabin you had out near the redwood forest?"

"It's still standing as far as I know. Fella I know rents it from me."

"Do you mean William Parker?" Gino asked sharply.

"That's him," Dan nodded. "Why?"

Gino told him about William Parker's demise. The old man hadn't heard about it.

"I never went there," Dan said. "You can say I as good as gave it to him. He took care of it. Said I didn't need to bother about it at all. Not that I get out of here much. I'm just biding my time now."

"Surely not," Anna clucked. "You seem to be in the pink of health."

"Can we go take a look at the cabin?" Gino asked. "What about a key?"

"Under the doormat as far as I know," Dan answered. "When you go, can you make sure the place is okay? Lock the windows and such? I might have to hire someone to look after it now that William is gone."

Gino promised to give Dan an update after they got back from the cabin. They said goodbye to the old man and walked out.

"Now what?" Anna asked.

"I would love to take you to lunch, Anna, but I have a meeting at the vineyard."

"Don't worry," Anna assured him. "I need to catch up with Cassie."

They parted ways, promising to talk later on the phone.

Chapter 20

Cassie went into her room and pulled out a box of frosted flakes from her closet. She was a grown woman hoarding cereal because her mother wouldn't let her eat the sugary treat. What had her life come to, Cassie thought with a shake of her head. She was going to eat two bowls of cereal and not feel guilty about it.

Cassie took her breakfast into the living room and switched the TV on, surfing to her favorite entertainment channel. She liked to catch up on what was going on in the lives of her peers. One of her rivals had been nominated for the Oscar a second time. Cassie wondered if she would ever get a chance to attend an awards function again, much less hold the coveted trophy in her hands.

Her cell phone rang and she picked it up eagerly, expecting Bobby. It turned out to be Teddy Fowler.

"Hey Teddy!" She was puzzled. What could Teddy want with her that early in the morning?

"Cassie, can you come to the police station?"

"Is something wrong with my mother?" Cassie asked in alarm.

Anna had gone out with Gino. So if something happened to her, shouldn't Gino be the one calling her, she wondered.

"We want to ask you a few questions."

"Are you making an official request, Teddy?" Cassie asked, finally catching up.

"Take it any way you like."

"Can't we talk about this, whatever this is, over lunch?"

"I'm afraid not. See you soon, Cassie. We are waiting."

Teddy offered to send a car for her but Cassie declined.

Cassie thought of calling Anna but decided against it. There was no point in bothering her without reason. Cassie pulled out the first dress she could lay her hands on and applied red lipstick for some courage. She spritzed some Joy perfume, slapped on a pair of dark shades and she was out of the door.

Teddy greeted her curtly when she reached the police station.

"What's the matter? Why are you so grim, Teddy?"

"I have to look official, Cassie. Everyone knows we are old friends. I can't be playing favorites."

Cassie stifled a grin and followed him into a room. A deputy was already in there.

"This is just routine, Ms. Butler," he said. "We are going to ask you a few questions."

"Do I need a lawyer?" Cassie asked.

"We haven't charged you with anything yet."

"Does that mean you are going to?"

The deputy refused to give her a straight answer. Cassie decided to wing it. She would stop talking to them the moment she felt uncomfortable.

"Teddy will be in here, won't he?"

"I can't, Cassie." Teddy grimaced. "There could be a conflict of interest."

"We are trying to establish your alibi for the night William Parker died," the deputy said. "Can you tell me where you were that evening?"

"I was at the Castle Beach Resort, of course. For that concert."

"Do you remember when you arrived there?"

Cassie thought a bit and gave an approximate time.

"Teddy should know. I was there with him and his wife."

"We have already talked to Detective Fowler about this. We just want to hear your version."

"I was with him," Cassie repeated. "Teddy had tickets to the concert and he invited me. Wanted to introduce me to his wife. She turned out to be a big fan of mine."

Cassie beamed at the police man, but he didn't drop his stern expression.

"What time did you leave the concert?"

"Right after it was over. Haven't you asked Teddy about it?"

The deputy cleared his throat.

"According to the detective, you were still at the hotel when he left with his wife. They had to go home early because of some domestic crisis."

"Oh yeah, right, now I remember. Their babysitter called. I don't know how people raise kids, really. They couldn't stay for the last set. It was the best one, you know. Before that, the singer was just warming up."

"Can anyone vouch for how long you remained at the hotel?" the deputy asked.

"I don't know. Someone must have seen me. Ask Charlie Robinson."

"Mr. Robinson and his staff are being interviewed," the deputy sighed. "Your story will be corroborated against what they tell us. But we want you to give us your version."

"If you're looking for the exact time I left, I'm sorry. I don't remember."

"One last question," the deputy said. "Did you notice a man with red hair and a Mohawk when you were at the concert?"

"Tall, rowdy man? He got into a fight with the bartender. Said his drink was watered or something."

"Do you know when he left?"

"Barely five minutes after the program started," Cassie said. "He was hard to miss."

"And when did you leave? Right after that?"

"Huh?" Cassie was flustered. "Are you trying to trap me or something? Didn't I just tell you I don't remember when I left?"

"Just checking," the deputy said lightly. "Based on the information we have, you could easily have poisoned the victim while he was at the concert."

"I didn't know he was there."

The deputy ignored that.

"We might call you in again, Ms. Butler."

Cassie let out a big breath after coming out of the room. Teddy was standing outside.

"That was brutal," she said. "Am I really a suspect, Teddy?"

"I can't comment on that, Cassie," he said. "It's best to come clean. The more forthcoming you are, the easier they will be on you. You can even cut a deal if you admit your mother coerced you into this."

"What a load of crap, Teddy! She did no such thing."

"I'm just trying to help."

"You call that helping? I thought you were my friend!"

Cassie pulled her phone out and saw she had missed a call from Anna. There was a message telling her Anna was waiting for her at home. Cassie rushed home, eager to tell her mother what had happened. She flew into Anna's arms as soon as she got home.

"I'm so scared, Mom."

"What happened?" Anna asked fearfully. "I've been worried about you, Cassie. Call it mother's intuition but I sensed you were in some kind of trouble."

"Teddy called me in for questioning. Only, he let someone else grill me."

Cassie poured out the whole story.

"What are we going to do now, Mom?"

"Don't worry about a thing, Cassie. I'm going to get to the bottom of this."

"Are you any closer to solving this, Mom?"

"It's hard to say. Frankly, I'm stumped. Ethan Lapin had a motive but he has a strong alibi."

"They asked me about some red headed guy," Cassie told her. "He was at the concert."

"Tall, hefty guy with red hair down the middle of his head? I don't remember what it's called."

"That's a Mohawk, Mom. And yes, that's the guy."

"That's Tim Buckner. Remember, I told you about him? I really think he and his son could be involved."

"What did you do today? Did you find that guy at the diner?"

"He turned out to be a journalist. He was following William Parker for a story. Gino is going to check up on him."

"What are you going to do now?"

"Bake," Anna said. "I need to distract myself. There are plenty of leftovers for lunch. Unless you want to go to the Tipsy Whale. If you do, get something for Meg too. She's alone at the store, poor thing."

Cassie declared she wasn't going anywhere.

"I shouldn't have lied to them about who closed up that night," Anna said. "Who's going to believe I'm telling the truth when they find out?"

"I know you did it for me, Mom. And I really don't remember leaving the door open. But I must have, right? I guess I was in a hurry to get to the resort on time. I should have double checked the lock."

"It's an old door," Anna said. "I think it will open if someone rattles it hard enough."

"What about those security tapes you found at the record store?" Cassie asked suddenly. "Have you told the police about them?"

Anna had forgotten about that.

"Let me call Teddy," Cassie said, pulling out her phone from her bag. "They might be able to test the lock and see how robust it is."

Cassie walked to her room as she talked to Ted. She collapsed on her bed, exhausted and emotional from her latest ordeal. Her hand groped under her bed, looking for the bottle she kept there for emergencies.

Chapter 21

Anna tasted the latest batch of cupcakes she had baked. She was pleased with her final tweak to the recipe and was ready to lock it down. She had come up with a strategy for the café. Every month, she would feature a different cupcake on the menu. It would be the Cupcake of the Month. It would highlight a fruit, preferably seasonal. And Anna would add her own twist to it, using a particular herb or spice.

Cassie came into the kitchen, followed by Gino. Anna urged both of them to try the cupcakes and give their genuine feedback. There was avocado toast for breakfast in case they got tired of eating the sweet stuff. Anna sprinkled some hot sauce on her own toast and listened to Gino and Cassie discuss some old Hollywood movie.

"I didn't know you were such a movie buff," she said to him. "You sound as bad as her."

"I have quite the collection," Gino boasted. "We should have a movie night sometime."

"What are you doing today, Mom?" Cassie wanted to know. "Heading to the store?"

"I'm going to check out that cabin Dan told us about," Gino told Anna. "Do you want to come with me?"

"Try holding me back," Anna said. "Just give me a few

minutes to get ready."

She pulled off her apron and went to her room. Five minutes later, she was ready for a morning out with Gino Mancini.

"I'll be home, in case you are wondering," Cassie said sullenly.

"You don't have to be," Anna clucked. "Why don't you go help Meg at the store?"

"I am expecting a call from my agent." Cassie supplied her favorite excuse.

"Suit yourself," Anna said and walked out.

Gino helped Anna into his truck and got in. He fiddled with the radio stations, trying to find something Anna liked.

"Tell me when to stop," he said. "I'm a country music fan myself."

"I don't mind country music," Anna said. "It can be very relaxing."

"You're a girl after my own heart, Anna Butler."

Anna blushed and began looking out of her window.

"Do you know where this cabin is?"

"I took the address from Dan the other day," Gino told her. "I know roughly where we are going. We might have to search a bit after that."

"Didn't you enter it into the navigation?" Anna asked.

"It's not on the map exactly," Gino explained. "We might have to walk a bit after we park the truck. I'll try to take us in as much as possible. The 4x4 will come in handy."

"I didn't realize it was that isolated."

"That's kind of the point, actually. I think I remember my Dad talking about it. He and Dan used to go there sometimes. It was a retreat of sorts for them. There's a creek nearby with plenty of trout. I might have gone there as a child. I have vague memories of standing in the water with a fishing rod in my hands. We cleaned that fish right there and grilled it on heated rocks."

"That's quite a story," Anna said. "You miss your father, don't you?"

Gino nodded.

"I'm a sentimental man, Anna. And I make no bones about it. I guess it's my Italian blood."

"I know men are supposed to find it hard to express themselves. But I appreciate a man who speaks from the heart. My John was like that."

They drove through towering redwoods on winding roads that took them further away from Dolphin Bay. Anna hadn't been out that way for a while. She sat back and enjoyed the view, wondering what they would find at the cabin.

Gino slowed down after a while and abruptly turned onto a

dirt road that was barely visible through the trees. It widened after they had gone a few meters and Anna was glad to see there was a road leading into the woods. Gino drove on until they came to a wide bank of pines and he could drive no more.

"I think this is where we get out."

He rushed to Anna's side and held her hand while she scrambled down. Gino put two bottles of water in a bag and hefted it on his shoulder.

"Better be prepared," he said to Anna. "We might not get a cell phone signal once we are surrounded by all these trees."

Anna felt a bit apprehensive. But Gino looked like he knew what he was doing. She was sure he would take care of them. Plus, she was curious about the cabin.

"Let's go," Gino said and led the way.

The ground was uneven, littered with stones and exposed roots. Someone had hacked a path through the trees and they followed it for ten minutes. Anna was going to suggest they turn back when they suddenly stepped into a clearing. Anna stared at the tumbledown structure that lay before them.

There was a scurrying sound and Anna cried out as a dark shadow flashed by. Footsteps faded in the distance.

"What was that? Did you see that, Gino?"

"I did," Gino answered grimly. "A bit too large to be a

chipmunk."

"Do you mean someone was inside that cabin?" Anna asked.

"I think they were trying to get inside. We must have spooked them. Do you prefer we go back, Anna?"

Anna hesitated. Clearly, someone else knew about the cabin. That meant the cabin was important. She didn't want to give up now.

"I think we need to go in."

The cabin was rugged and dilapidated. Years of neglect were evident in its appearance. Anna wondered why Dan or William Parker hadn't spared a lick of paint for the cabin over the years.

"Here we go," Gino said and walked up the steps.

There was a cracking sound and his foot went in as the decaying wood gave way.

"Gino! Are you alright?" Anna cried.

Gino had grabbed the railing. He pulled his foot out gingerly and rotated his ankle.

"No harm done, I think."

Anna stepped forward hesitantly and went up the steps without incident. Gino had already pulled up the doormat per Dan's instructions and found the key. He inserted it in the rusty lock and jiggled it a bit to open the door.

The inside was musty as Anna had expected. A hearth held the remains of a fire. There was an old leather sofa placed along a wall, faded and torn with stuffing coming out. A bookcase lined the other wall, sparsely stacked with some tattered volumes. Anna was sure they would fall apart when touched.

Gino stamped the floor with his foot and tapped the walls.

"Something's not right."

"What do you mean?" Anna asked.

"This room is smaller than it should be. The cabin looks much bigger from the outside."

"I think you're right," Anna said, looking out toward the length of the porch.

Gino lifted some of the books and tapped the back of the bookshelf. He exclaimed in surprise.

"Can you lend me a hand, Anna? Let's try to move this."

To Gino's surprise, the bookshelf moved aside easily.

"It's on wheels," Gino cried.

He moved the bookshelf out of the way and stumbled into a room that had been hidden from them.

"Wow!" Anna muttered as she looked around.

They were in a cavernous space, bigger than the living room or whatever room they had been in. An old cherry desk sat in the center of the room with a tufted leather chair behind it. Both the desk and the chair were in excellent condition, unlike the rest of the furniture in the cabin. An old computer sat on the desk.

"This is some hideout," Anna said. "My guess is your friend Dan knows nothing about this."

"I agree with you, Anna. Looks like William Parker made himself at home here."

Gino started taking pictures of the room.

"Over here, Gino." Anna stared at a wall that had been hidden in the shadows.

A large cork board was mounted on the wall, taking up most of the available space. It was pinned with newspaper clippings, old photos and handwritten notes.

Gino made sure he took pictures of the board.

"I think I'll have some of that water now," Anna said weakly.

Gino pulled out a bottle of water and handed it to her.

"We have definitely stumbled on to something, Anna. I think we should head back now, before it gets too late."

"Do you think that journalist guy has been here before us?"

"I have no idea," Gino said.

"What about that person we saw when we got here?"

"Maybe it was just some wild animal," Gino mused.

He followed Anna out of the room and repositioned the bookshelf to hide the inner space. He locked the front door after they stepped out and pocketed the key.

"I think I'll keep this with me for now. Dan won't mind, I'm sure."

"Are you planning to come back here?" Anna asked.

"I need to take a look at that computer," Gino said.

"What does all this mean, Gino?" Anna asked on the way back to the truck. "Do you think this has anything to do with William Parker?"

Gino's jaw hardened as they reached his 4x4.

"Take it from this old cop, Anna. I'm positive it has everything to do with him."

Chapter 22

Anna rearranged the cushions one more time and breathed deeply as she looked around the café. She was already beginning to feel proud of the place and was looking forward to making it a success. It would be a one of its kind café in Dolphin Bay. Between the locals and the tourists that traveled along the Pacific Coast Highway, she was sure she could get plenty of business.

"It's looking good," Meg said from behind her. "Aren't you tired of moving these things around again and again?"

"I want it to be perfect," Anna said.

Meg had surprised her with her hard work and attention to detail. She had transformed the bookstore since the few days she had been working there. Anna was proud of her too. Someone had raised that girl right. Then she sobered as she realized Meg had probably raised herself.

"Have you talked to your parents lately, Meg? How are they?"

"They are good," Meg replied. "They are traveling to Japan next week. My Dad's office is sending him there for a conference. They are going to stay on for a week after that and travel around."

"They must be worried about you."

Meg gave a tiny shrug.

"Not really. I told them you are looking after me."

"You got that right, sweetie."

Anna started straightening up the bookstore. Meg put the books back on the shelves and dusted everything. Soon they were ready to leave for the day.

"I don't know how you do it, but sales have improved since you started working here."

"People are getting excited about the café," Meg told her. "Things will improve a lot once the café is up and running."

"I guess I will have to order more books from the bestseller lists," Anna thought out loud.

She gathered her purse and bid Meg goodnight.

"I'm right behind you," Meg said. "I just want to finish entering some of these old romance titles into the system."

"You will have to teach me what you are doing some day."

Anna walked out and picked up her bike. It was a windy evening, just warm enough to enjoy the salty breeze whipping her hair around. A mosaic of pink and orange covered the sky. There were a lot of people on the Coastal Walk, out with their pets or sitting on the benches, eating ice cream and watching the sun set over the bay. Anna smiled and started pedaling home.

She felt herself topple almost the same moment she heard the roar of a motor and a jarring screech of tires on the asphalt. For a split second, she wondered if it was Cassie driving her Mercedes. The next moment she was on the ground, shaking in fear as an unfamiliar car zoomed past her.

A couple of people from the Coastal Walk ran to help her. Meg came running out of the store. The next few minutes were a blur to Anna. Meg must have helped her up and taken her back into the store. Anna found a glass of water thrust into her hands.

"What was that jerk thinking?" Meg fumed. "You could have been hurt. Really hurt."

"I'm not sure what happened, exactly. Did I pass out?"

"I don't know," Meg said. "I'm calling the police."

"Is that necessary?" Anna asked.

Given her recent history, she wasn't sure the police would be on her side.

Meg dialed the emergency number and told them what had happened. She made some sugary coffee and forced Anna to drink it.

A deputy arrived fifteen minutes later. He noted the bruise on Anna's cheek.

"Did anyone assault you, Ma'am?"

"She got that when she hit the ground," Meg explained.

"The car was speeding. The driver didn't actually hit Anna but he was too close. She lost her balance and fell."

"Do you think he wanted to hit you?" The cop looked at Anna.

Anna felt bewildered. "It all happened too fast. I'm still trying to wrap my head around it."

Meg explained where the car had come from.

"Isn't this part of Main Street supposed to be a No Drive zone?"

"That's right," the deputy nodded. "The spot you mention is part of the Downtown Loop. Most of the locals know they can't bring their cars in here. It's been like that for years."

"Are you saying this reckless driver was from out of town?" Anna asked.

"Hard to say at this point," the deputy answered. "Did you get a look at him, Miss?" he asked Meg.

"I got a fleeting glimpse. I don't think I will be able to recognize him if I saw him again."

"Can you describe him?"

"He was a young kid, about my age. Early twenties maybe?"

"Was he local? What about the car?"

"I'm new in town," Meg explained. "So I couldn't say."

The deputy offered to call the paramedics or give Anna a ride to the hospital.

"You need to get that cleaned up."

"I can do it at home," Anna assured him. "Thank you for your support, Officer."

"I'm taking you home," Meg said sternly as soon as the policeman left. "Can you walk or should I call Cassie?"

"We'll walk," Anna said quickly. "No need to worry her."

Anna summoned an inner store of energy she didn't know she had. The walk seemed to drag on forever. Meg kept her entertained with stories of people who had come to the bookstore in the past few days.

Cassie sprang up from the couch when they entered the house.

"Is something wrong, Mom?"

"Anna had a little accident," Meg told her. "Some kid in a car almost ran her down."

"Where were you when this happened?" Cassie demanded. "Couldn't you have protected her or something?"

"Meg was wrapping up in the store," Anna said. "Calm down, Cassie. No reason to get all het up."

"You're hurt, Mom." Cassie must have noticed the bruise on Anna's cheek.

"Do you have a first aid kit?" Meg asked, urging Anna to sit down and put her feet up.

Cassie came out with some cotton and antiseptic. Meg took over. She cleaned up the bruise and put a Band-Aid on it.

"Tell me everything," Cassie ordered. "Don't leave anything out."

The doorbell rang. Cassie went to open the door. Gino stood outside, carrying a large canvas bag in his arms.

"I come bearing gifts," he said. "Where is she? Is she okay, Cassie?"

"You know."

"I heard about it on the police scanner. I wanted to make sure Anna's fine."

"What's in the bag?"

"I brought dinner. Food is the best cure for shock. It's my special pot roast with fixings."

"Meg's here too," Cassie said, walking back to the living room.

"There's enough for everyone," Gino assured her.

Anna was surprised to see Gino. He fussed over her, making sure she had enough cushions and suggesting she see a doctor anyway.

"I don't like this, Anna," Gino said. "What have you done

since yesterday?"

"Nothing much. I was in the store all day today."

"I don't think this was an accident."

"What do you mean, Gino?" Cassie asked, aghast. "You're saying someone hit her on purpose?"

"I didn't actually get hit," Anna corrected her.

"Is that supposed to make me feel better?" Cassie muttered.

Anna rubbed her forehead and sighed.

"Can we eat? I feel a headache coming on."

They all trooped into the kitchen. Anna was relieved to see Cassie pulling out plates and silverware. She told her to serve the food.

They sat around the small kitchen table, enjoying the hearty pot roast with roasted potatoes and a red wine pan gravy that was Gino's specialty.

"I spoke to Teddy Fowler about your little accident," Gino told Anna. "I hope you don't mind."

"What for?"

"I think this was a deliberate attack and I made sure Teddy knew it," Gino told them. "Although I am not crazy about what happened, it does work in your favor, Anna."

"How so?" she asked.

"It means you are getting close. You have scared someone. I think he or she was trying to warn you to stay away."

"It was definitely a guy," Meg said.

"Does this let us off the hook?" Cassie asked eagerly. "Will the police stop thinking we had anything to do with William Parker?"

"Teddy didn't say that right away, but I think I have got him thinking in the right direction," Gino told her.

"That was nice of you, Gino," Anna said. "You think this happened because we went to that cabin?"

Gino shrugged.

"We need to go back there and look at that computer."

Anna looked at Meg.

"I know you have been doing some fancy stuff on that old computer at the bookstore. Are you some kind of tech wiz?"

"More of a geek, I guess," Meg owned up. "I took some advanced courses in computers. Network security, ethical hacking, that kind of stuff."

"Sounds like Greek and Latin to me," Anna grunted. "But you might be able to help us."

"We sure could use your help, Meg," Gino nodded. "I

would rather not ask an outsider at this point."

"Cassie can manage the bookstore tomorrow," Anna said. "We are going to the cabin."

"Wait a minute," Cassie cried. "I want to see this cabin."

Anna rolled her eyes.

"Don't be a crybaby. You can go there some other time."

"That's settled, then," Gino said, playing peacemaker between mother and daughter. "I think it's time to call it a night, Anna. We have a big day tomorrow."

Chapter 23

Anna woke up feeling refreshed. She had slept well and was ready to face the day. She was surprised to see Cassie in the kitchen.

"Here you go, Mom," Cassie said, placing a steaming cup of coffee before her. "Freshly ground beans, brewed just the way you like."

Anna thanked her and took a sip of the delicious coffee.

"Are you sleepwalking or something, Cassie?"

"Laugh all you want. I am making breakfast today. My famous cheese omelets with fresh orange juice and sourdough French Toast."

Anna wasn't sure Cassie could manage all that but she smiled encouragingly.

"I'm making enough for Meg, don't worry," Cassie told her. "I asked her to come and eat here."

"You've been busy," Anna observed.

"I can't send you off to the jungle without a proper breakfast, can I?"

"It's not that far from town," Anna said. "But thanks, Cassie."

Meg came in through the kitchen door. Anna greeted her and smiled when Meg hugged her.

"Did you sleep well, Anna?" she asked. "We should change your dressing before we go out."

"Don't worry," Anna said. "I think it's already dried up."

Anna was upbeat as they sat at the kitchen table, devouring the food. Cassie sat on her left and Meg on her right. She could almost believe they were one happy family.

Gino arrived just as they finished eating. He assured Anna he had breakfasted before starting from home.

"How far is this cabin?" Meg asked as they set off in Gino's truck.

"About half an hour by car and fifteen or twenty minutes by foot," Gino told her.

Anna wished the Firecrackers were going with her.

"I talked to Julie last night. She really wanted to come but she's on a strict deadline. Mary's gone to San Jose. Her daughter isn't feeling too good and needs some help with the kids."

"You miss your friends," Gino observed.

"We have always hung out together," Anna told him. "I don't know what I would have done without them these past two years. Cassie was home of course, but there are some things I can't share with her."

"Like what?" Meg asked. "Do you mean you two aren't close?"

Anna swallowed a lump as she saw the wide eyed curiosity Meg displayed.

"It's not that," she said hastily. "It's hard to explain, sweetie. You'll understand when you are my age."

"That's what grownups always say when they don't want to give a straight answer," Meg said with a smirk.

"We're almost there," Gino announced as he took the little turnoff and eased his car onto the dirt road.

They got out a few minutes later and started walking. Meg gave a low whistle when she saw the cabin.

"Why would anyone want to live here?" she wondered out loud.

"Wait till we get inside," Gino laughed.

Meg's eyes popped when Gino wheeled the bookshelf away from the wall to reveal the room inside.

"Whoever did this was up to no good," Meg observed. "Why go to so much trouble to hide this space?"

Anna pointed toward the computer that sat on the desk.

"We are hoping to find an answer there."

"All yours, kiddo," Gino said. "Try to work your magic."

Meg sat down in the chair and tapped a few keys. Anna watched the computer screen light up after a while.

"My guess is we are going to need a password," Meg said. "Do you know anything about the person who used this computer? His name, date of birth, the names of his pets or family members?"

"As far as I know, William Parker lived alone," Anna said. "He did have a family but they left him long ago."

Meg was looking through a stack of files on the desk. She opened some drawers and rifled through them. Anna saw her smile.

"This may be it," Meg said, ripping something off the inside of a drawer.

She waved a tiny slip of paper that seemed to be torn off a Post-it note.

"Does it work?" Anna asked eagerly as Meg typed the letters from the piece of paper into the computer.

"Awesome!" Meg crowed as the home screen appeared on the computer. "I'm in."

Gino had been standing in front of the cork board, studying the photos and news clippings.

"What have you got there, Gino?" Anna asked.

"You remember I took pictures of this board the last time we were here? I have been studying them a bit."

"Anything interesting about them?"

"They seem to be news items related to old murder cases from around the country."

"That's odd," Anna said. "What was Parker doing with them?"

There was a thud outside. Anna remembered how Gino's foot had gone through the rotten porch step.

"Someone's coming," Gino whispered, warning Anna to be quiet with a finger on his lips.

He rushed outside just as a man came in, muttering a string of curses.

"Stop right there!" Gino commanded in a stern voice that meant business. "This is private property."

"Joey Bellinger!" Anna exclaimed as she recognized the journalist they had met at the diner. "What are you doing here?"

Joey planted his feet wide and folded his hands.

"This is not your property," he challenged Gino.

"I have permission from the owner to be here. I can bet a case of my latest vintage that you don't."

"Look, I'm just working on my story."

"You are a freelancer who hasn't published anything under his byline in three years," Gino said.

"So you checked up on me," Joey sighed. "I shouldn't have expected anything less from a former police chief."

"How did you find this cabin?" Anna asked Joey. "Did someone tell you about it?"

"I followed Parker," Joey admitted. "He used to come here almost every day."

"What is your interest in William Parker?" Gino asked. "Do you know he died recently?"

Joey told them he knew about it.

"Did you come to Dolphin Bay before that?" Gino asked. "How do we know you didn't have a motive to kill him?"

"William Parker was a bad man," Joey said. "A dangerous man. Whoever killed him did the world a favor, believe me."

"We know he was disliked by most," Anna told him. "Why did you hate him?"

"I didn't have any particular feelings for him. He was just the subject of my investigation."

"Care to elaborate more?" Gino asked.

"I can't," Joey said with a shrug. "Not without compromising what I am working on. As you said, I've been at it for three years."

Anna saw Gino hesitate.

"I'm going to go with my gut feel and let you in," Gino said. "Tell me what you make of this."

He led Joey Bellinger to the cork board. Anna saw Joey's mouth drop open in surprise. She walked over to the board and began reading, trying to make some sense out of it.

"From your expression, I think you have seen some of this before," Gino said, narrowing his eyes at Joey.

"You are right," Joey sighed. "It kind of confirms my theory. That's all I can tell you right now."

"There's a common thread here," Anna commented, moving closer to read something in really fine print. "All these people were acquitted, Gino. I guess they were wrongly accused."

"Or they had really good lawyers," Gino offered. "That's a smart observation, Anna. I don't know how I missed that."

"You would have caught it sooner or later," Anna soothed. "Where do you think these people are now?"

"I am more curious to know why Parker had them on this board," Gino quipped. He turned to Joey. "Anna is a suspect in William Parker's murder. I believe she is innocent. If you have any information that will help us exonerate her, I urge you to reveal it. You don't have to tell us. You can go directly to the police."

"I'll think about it," Joey promised them and left the cabin.

"I can't figure him out," Anna said. "And I am not sure we can rule him out as a suspect."

"You're right, Anna. Let's go see what Meg's been up to."

Meg was sitting back in the armchair with her hands behind her head. She looked like the cat that swallowed the canary.

"You are looking quite pleased," Anna said. "Did you find something useful on that computer?"

"I can tell you what I found," Meg said, getting up to stretch. "There's a bunch of files which look like accounts related to a business. Some emails with someone who could be his son. And one more thing ...whoever used this computer was very fond of chess."

"Chess?" Gino asked. "What makes you say that?"

"The logs show he used to play chess on the Internet and chat with someone."

"That sounds encouraging, Meg," Gino said. "Did you read the messages?"

Meg nodded.

"They make absolutely no sense."

Chapter 24

At the bookstore, Cassie dusted some shelves halfheartedly, mulling over the conversation she had just had with her agent. She had been offered a small role in an indie film. It felt like a slap in the face to Cassie. The filmmaker, a recent film school graduate, thought she was perfect for the role of a fifty year old matriarch. He couldn't afford to pay her, of course. Cassie had given her agent a piece of her mind. He told her she couldn't expect anything more after her long hiatus from Hollywood.

Cassie sat at the reading table near the windows, staring out at the bay. The bell over the door jingled and Julie swept in.

"I thought you were working on a deadline," Cassie exclaimed.

"I was," Julie nodded with a grimace. "Or I am supposed to be, but my mind's buzzing with too many ideas. I needed a break."

"We can't leave the store but we can talk here."

"Tell me some latest gossip," Julie cajoled. "I can use a laugh."

"The gossip is that I have become a laughing stock myself." Cassie told her about her conversation with her agent.

"Fire that ingrate and get a new agent," Julie advised. "You don't work for them. They work for you. Show them who's the boss."

"But I've been with this agency for ten years," Cassie cried.

"That's why they are taking you for granted. Believe me, I've been there."

Julie was a popular author who had sold millions of books so Cassie trusted her. She promised to consider her advice.

"How's Anna recovering from last night?"

"She seemed fine this morning," Cassie said. "I invited Meg for breakfast to cheer Mom up."

"That was nice of you, sweetie. How are you getting along with her?"

"Okay, I guess." Cassie dodged the question.

"Alright, I get the message." Julie didn't press her. "Let's go to the Tipsy Whale for lunch. They are having those roast turkey and avocado sandwiches today, with the pepper bacon."

"That sounds yum!" Cassie smacked her lips. "But it's barely 10 AM, Aunt Julie."

"I don't need a time to talk about food," Julie laughed. "I think I have a problem."

They both looked up at the same time when the bell behind the door jingled again. Teddy Fowler came in, looking grim.

"Hey Teddy!" Cassie greeted him. "Are you here to pick up those books your wife wanted?"

"I'm here on official business," Teddy said. "You need to come with me, Cassie."

"What's going on, Detective?" Julie stood up.

"I am here to arrest Cassie for the murder of William Parker." He looked at Cassie. "I hope you will come without a fuss. I really don't want to handcuff you."

"Wha … what are you talking about, Teddy?" Cassie croaked.

Her face had paled and her eyes were wide with disbelief.

"Go with him now," Julie advised. "I'm calling Anna. We'll be right behind you, don't worry."

Cassie nodded mutely and followed Teddy Fowler out of the store. She didn't say a word on the way to the police station. Teddy took her to a bare room and left her there. He came back after what seemed like ages with a deputy in tow.

"Why have you arrested me?" Cassie demanded, finally finding her voice. "I'm innocent."

"The evidence is stacked against you, Cassie," Teddy explained. "You were at the bookstore during the time Parker was killed. We also have proof you went there after the concert."

"So what?" Cassie challenged.

"That means you were present at the scene of the crime," the deputy said. "You have a motive and an opportunity."

"Can you prove I poisoned the man?" Cassie asked.

Teddy looked sad.

"The final reports have come in. William Parker died from a blow to his head. The poison just knocked him out. There are plenty of heavy books in that store, Cassie, as you very well know. You could have hit him with any one of them."

"Where is it, then?" Cassie demanded. "Show me this weapon."

"You could have chucked it anywhere. Or just put it back on some bookshelf."

"That's your best theory?" Cassie scoffed. "You know me, Teddy. You have known me since we were kids. Do you really think I could do something like this?"

"My opinion doesn't matter, Cassie," Teddy sighed. "And there are no other suspects."

"That's where you are wrong," Cassie said calmly. "What about Tim Buckner, huh?"

"Tim Buckner has an alibi," the deputy said. "And he had no reason to hurt William Parker. Any association they might have had ended a long time ago. Now Tim has a business in Blackberry Beach. He's doing his own thing away from Dolphin Bay."

"Obviously, you don't know the whole story," Cassie

scoffed.

"What are you implying, Cassie?" Teddy asked.

"I met William Parker's lawyer," she told him. "Parker and Buckner had a falling out, right? Buckner accused Parker of embezzling money from the business. Parker threw it back at him and said Buckner was the one stealing the money. Nothing was really proved so they closed the business and Buckner set up his own gig in Blackberry Beach with his son."

"We know all that," the deputy said with a smirk.

"It seems Parker still held a grudge against Tim Buckner. The Buckners were doing good in the neighboring town. Parker's reputation suffered though and he wasn't doing that great here in Dolphin Bay. He blamed it all on Buckner."

"Where's the motive, Cassie?" Teddy prompted.

"I'm coming to it," Cassie said patiently. "The lawyer told me Parker wanted to go after his old partner and sue for damages. He was preparing a big lawsuit against him. It had potential to wipe out the Buckners. According to the lawyer, Parker had a good chance of winning."

"You are suggesting Tim Buckner got wind of this." Teddy was thoughtful.

"It's possible, isn't it?" Cassie argued. "I call that a motive."

There was some kind of altercation outside and Cassie thought she heard Anna's voice.

"My Mom's here," she sighed with relief.

Teddy went outside, talking to the deputy under his breath. Cassie crossed her fingers and waited. He came back in after another lifetime.

"They are letting you go now, Cassie."

Cassie jumped up and scrambled out of the room.

Anna was waiting outside with Gino. She opened her arms wide and Cassie ran into them.

"Oh Mom, it was horrible!"

"My poor baby," Anna said, her eyes welling up. "Let's go home now. We can talk later."

Julie and Meg were pacing outside the station. They broke into smiles when they saw Cassie. Julie hugged her first and then Meg moved in for a hug. Cassie felt a curious warmth as the young girl wrapped her arms around her.

"Are you alright?" Meg asked, looking into her eyes.

"I'm fine," Cassie dismissed.

Gino had to go back to the vineyard. He promised to catch up with them later. Julie drove them all home in her SUV. Anna started a pot of coffee and set out a platter of cookies and cupcakes.

"I must have said something convincing," Cassie said as she ate some frosting off an orange cupcake. "They actually let me go."

"Gino had something to do with it," Anna told her.

"That sweet man!" Cassie exclaimed. "I need to thank him right now, Mom. What did he do?"

"You can say he pulled some strings. He spoke with the current police chief. Gino convinced him there was more than one suspect out there. I did my bit too. Promised him all kinds of consequences if he didn't release you."

"Do you think Lara Crawford had anything to do with Cassie's arrest?" Julie asked them.

Anna shook her head. "I don't think so." She turned toward Cassie. "They mentioned you had gone back to the store that night. What were you doing there, Cassie?"

"I thought I might have left the door open."

"But the door was open the next morning," Anna said, puzzled.

Cassie looked sheepish.

"Bobby called me just as I reached the store. I turned around to talk to him and walked back to my car. I think I forgot why I went there."

Cassie didn't want to admit she had imbibed a bit at the bar earlier that evening.

"How is your search for the real culprit going, Anna?" Julie asked. "Time's running out."

Cassie closed her eyes and took a few deep breaths, trying

to relax. Her tryst at the police station had shaken her. She wasn't ready to go through the harrowing experience again.

"She's right, Mom. We need to find out what happened to William Parker."

Chapter 25

Anna slid the chicken breasts into the oven, smothered in her special tomato sauce and lots of fresh mozzarella cheese. She was making Chicken Parmesan as a 'Welcome Home' dinner for Cassie.

"Something smells awesome, Mom." Cassie came into the kitchen, freshly showered, casually dressed in a pair of shorts and a tank top.

"I'm making your favorite dinner – Chicken Parmesan with Spaghetti and tiramisu for dessert."

"With lots of garlic bread?"

"Of course." Anna smiled. "I would never make an Italian meal without garlic bread."

"Where's Meg?"

"I invited her to stay over tonight. She's gone back to Mary's to get some clothes."

"I hope Gino's coming to dinner? I haven't had a chance to thank him properly yet."

The doorbell rang just then. Anna rushed to the front door and came back with Gino in tow. He was carrying two bottles of wine.

"These will go great with whatever you're making."

"You're spoiling us with all this great wine, Gino," Anna grumbled goodnaturedly. "Soon you won't have any left for yourself."

Gino laughed.

"Have you forgotten? I have a cellar full of this. And the new vintage will soon be bottled later this year."

Cassie uncorked the wine and let it breathe. Anna had made some caprese salad as an appetizer. She set it out, along with some juicy melon wrapped in prosciutto.

"How are you holding up, Cassie?" Gino asked. "I'm sorry you had to go through all that today. The police can be a bit bullheaded sometimes."

"I'm better now, thanks to you." Cassie was effusive in her gratitude. "How can I make it up to you?"

"Come to my house for movie night. I'll have the popcorn ready."

Cassie promised they would set it up soon.

Meg walked in through the kitchen door and headed straight for the canapés.

"I'm starving," she apologized to Anna after eating a couple of the melon chunks.

"Don't spoil your appetite, then. Dinner's ready."

William Parker was forgotten as they all exclaimed over the food and tucked in. There was plenty to go around but every pot and pan was scraped clean.

"That was delicious, Anna," Gino said. "Thank you. I'm going to put on some pounds if I keep eating here."

Meg looked happy too.

"I second Gino. You're a fantastic cook, Anna."

"My mother taught me," Anna said proudly. "And my Nona."

They filed into the living room, agreeing they needed some time before they could tackle dessert.

The mood in the room went down a notch when Gino told them what he had been doing all day.

"I found something shocking. Don't know how it fits in with our little case."

Gino had spent the day at the police station, doing some research. He had looked into the clippings they had seen on the cork board at the cabin. Anna's observation about all of them being set free had got him going.

"What do you mean, they are all dead?" Anna asked, stunned. "Were they old?"

"Some of them were," Gino nodded, "but not old enough to die."

"What happened to them?" Meg asked.

"Believe it or not, they all suffered some kind of accident." Gino looked around, noting their reactions.

"That sounds fishy," Anna said immediately. "What are the odds?"

"Slim." Gino agreed. "I have been trying to make sense of it."

Anna was mulling over the information in her mind. Her eyes widened as she thought about something.

"So are you saying someone has been deliberately wiping these people out?"

"Vigilante justice!" Meg exclaimed. "That's unreal, dude."

"We don't know that yet," Gino warned. "Let's not get ahead of ourselves."

Anna was frowning as she tried to process everything.

"What does William Parker have to do with all this? Where does he fit in?"

"You knew him, Anna. Did he seem like the righteous type? Someone who would take the law in his own hands?"

"I barely remember him," Anna stressed. "I couldn't say either way."

"If Parker was responsible for harming these people, it changes everything." Gino stood up and began pacing the room. "He could be a target, Anna."

"What does this mean for me?" Cassie asked. "Does it mean there are more suspects?"

"If what we think is true, there could be any number of suspects out there," Gino explained. "It will be almost impossible to track them down."

"As long as it gets the focus away from Cassie," Anna said. "Have you told the police about this, Gino?"

"Not yet. I'm still trying to wrap my head around it. I don't want to go to them with some fantastic theory and get laughed at."

Anna knew Gino had been a highly respected police chief for several years. He had a certain reputation to uphold.

"We need to do some preliminary research ourselves, Gino." Anna looked formidable as she came to a decision. "That's the only way to ensure they won't take my little girl away again."

"Little girl?" Cassie objected. "Mom!"

"You're so fortunate," Meg said. "You have a mother who will do anything for you."

Anna felt her eyes well up.

"Time for cake," she said and hurried into the kitchen before anyone could notice her tears.

They were all quiet while they dug into Anna's famous tiramisu.

"I think I need to sleep on this," Gino said after he had reluctantly said no to a second helping. "I'm exhausted."

"We are all tired," Anna agreed. "It's been a helluva day."

They all said goodbye to Gino.

"I really appreciate everything you are doing for us," Anna told him as she saw him out. "I don't know how I can ever repay you."

"We are friends, aren't we?" Gino asked softly. "This is what friends do for each other."

The climbing rose near Anna's front door was redolent with a sweet scent. The summer evening had turned cooler and a starry night bathed them in a silvery light.

Anna impulsively hugged Gino and sprang back, trying to hide a blush.

"I'll be seeing you, Anna Butler."

Gino turned around and walked to his truck. Anna stood there long after his tail lights disappeared in the distance.

"Are you mooning over Gino?" Cassie whispered in her ear.

Anna jumped. She opened her mouth to protest but stopped at the sound of Meg's laughter.

"She's just teasing you, Anna."

They all went inside and took a second helping of the cake,

giving in to temptation.

"I brought my sleeping bag," Meg told Anna. "Can I roll it out here?"

"Oh honey, you don't need a sleeping bag." Anna felt nervous. "I have a guest room. Your bed is ready for you."

"Are you sure?" Meg asked. "I'm used to camping out in my sleeping bag."

"Not tonight," Anna said firmly. "Let your old grandmother pamper you a bit."

Anna noticed Cassie was looking uncomfortable. She changed the subject and asked if anyone wanted coffee.

"I prefer hot chocolate before going to bed," Meg said shyly.

"We can all have some hot cocoa later then," Anna said. "I know everyone is tired but I'm too full to sleep right away."

"Me too," Meg said. "But I would like to change into my jammies if you don't mind."

Anna took Meg to the room she had prepared for her.

"It's such a soothing color," Meg said, looking around the room with pleasure. "Lavender is my favorite color." She admired the large canvas mounted over the bed. "I love sunflowers! Did you paint this yourself, Anna?"

"I couldn't paint to save my life," Anna laughed. "We bought that in France. John and I went there one summer.

We spent two fabulous weeks in the South of France."

Meg opened the backpack she was carrying and pulled out a set of pajamas. Anna stood up to leave.

"Don't go, Anna," Meg said. "I can change in the closet."

She came out two minutes later, dressed in pink pajamas covered in yellow duckies. Anna wove her arm around Meg's and kissed her.

"Are you ready for that cocoa now?"

Chapter 26

Cassie felt a bit out of her depth as she sat in the living room with Anna and Meg. It was a cozy scene. They were all dressed in their night things and Anna had lit the fire in the grate. Cassie thought it was surreal, like a scene in a fairy tale. Anna and Meg were talking nineteen to the dozen, bonding over little things. Cassie felt like an outsider among them.

She had been shocked when Meg pulled out her sleeping bag. What kind of life had that girl led? Cassie thought she was at least partly responsible for whatever had happened to Meg. Would she ever forgive her?

"Cassie likes the mini marshmallows too," Anna was telling Meg. "She won't drink her hot chocolate without them. And oh yes, there have to be seven marshmallows in her cup. Not six or eight. Seven. Go figure."

"I always add an even number," Meg said with a laugh. "I can't explain it."

"We should make s'mores," Anna said. "But I don't have the energy or the room in my stomach. We'll do it the next time you stay over."

Cassie yawned widely.

"It's getting late, you two. Why don't we just go to bed?"

"I'm going to look up some things on my laptop," Meg said. "You can turn in, Cassie. You had quite the day."

"I'll stay with you, Meg," Anna said. "We can run some searches together."

"Now you are making me feel bad," Cassie sighed. "You are doing all this for me, so I guess I should at least stick around."

Anna told Meg to bring her laptop out to the living room.

"Where should we start?" Meg asked. "Any ideas, Anna?"

"We need to make a list of all the victims first," Anna replied.

"That's a lot of people," Meg said. "Why don't we consider a radius around Dolphin Bay?"

"Good point," Anna said.

Meg made a list of the people on the computer, then sorted them based on their distance from Dolphin Bay. She made a shorter list of people who had lived in a 300 mile radius.

"7 people?" Anna asked. "That's a lot for our neck of the woods."

Cassie was looking over Meg's shoulder, trying to understand what she was doing. She had never grasped the concept of spreadsheets so it was all a bit too much for her.

"What about the timeframe?" she wondered out loud. "Did all these people die recently?"

Meg did a quick check and shook her head.

"Anywhere from last year to ten years ago. There doesn't seem to be any pattern here."

"Let's look all of them up one by one," Anna said.

Meg nodded and picked up the first name on the list.

"This is a 25 year old woman whose toddler died in an accident. She was crossing the road with him when she dropped her bag. She bent down to pick it up. Her grip on her baby boy must have loosened. The next thing she knew, he was ten meters from her, run over by a car."

"That sounds horrific," Cassie exclaimed. "Poor woman."

"It could have happened to anyone," Anna mused. "Did they arrest her?"

Meg read off the screen.

"She was accused of neglect and charged with manslaughter. Public opinion was largely against her. The media crucified her. People blamed her for the loss of an innocent life."

"I feel sorry for that woman. She must have gone through hell."

"Did she go to prison?" Cassie asked.

"Jury let her go," Meg said, reading off the screen. "She was asked to go for some kind of therapy. That's it."

"How did she die?" Anna asked, trying to remember.

"Accident," Meg replied. "She was run over by a car in the middle of the street in broad daylight."

"Sounds like poetic justice," Cassie murmured. "Or a bad horror movie."

"What about her family?" Anna asked. "Did anyone support her through the trial?"

"Doesn't look like it," Meg said. "Her husband abandoned her. He got married a month after she died. That's all I can find out right now."

"When and where did this happen?" Anna asked.

Meg mentioned a suburb in the Bay Area. The young mother had died three years ago.

"If there's a connection with Parker here, I don't see it," Anna said. "Let's move on to the next one, Meg."

Meg poured out another shocking story.

"What do you mean, the woman killed herself?" Cassie asked.

"The guy on our list supposedly abused her. Some women's group forced the woman to sue him. It was a big scandal and people were judgmental. Some said it was her fault. The woman couldn't take all the unwanted attention so she committed suicide."

"What about the man on our list?" Anna asked.

"He was just in the wrong place at the wrong time. They didn't have any actual evidence against him so he was let go."

"What happened to him?" Cassie asked, leaning forward in anticipation.

"He went missing," Meg told them. "His body was found in some woods a year later, identified based on dental records."

Anna and Cassie grew increasingly sober as Meg narrated a few more stories.

"Stop!" Cassie exclaimed, holding her hand up. "I've had enough of this. It's just too depressing."

"I have to agree with you, Cassie," Anna said. "I'm going to have nightmares for a week."

"I find it very confusing," Meg told them. "I mean, who's the bad guy here. It's hard to say."

"I think your theory about vigilante justice was correct, Meg," Anna said thoughtfully. "The court may have let these people go, but someone thought they didn't deserve to live. They took the law in their own hands and decided to get rid of these people."

"How could they be sure, Anna?" Meg asked.

"These people have big egos, I guess," Anna offered. "They are sure what they think is right, and they want to enforce it on everyone else."

"But that's cruel!" Meg exclaimed.

"I think it's time we all turned in," Anna said, coaxing Meg to shut down her laptop. "Promise me you won't be looking at it any more, young lady!"

"I know that tone," Cassie said. "You don't want to cross her when she talks like that, Meg."

"Okay, okay." Meg laughed easily. "I'll keep my laptop right here on the coffee table."

They bid each other goodnight and went to their rooms. Cassie hesitated outside Meg's room.

"You'll be alright, won't you, Meg?" she asked her, peeping in.

"I'm a pretty sound sleeper," Meg assured her. "Once I'm out, nothing can wake me up."

Cassie slept fitfully that night. She finally got up when the first rays of the sun filtered into her room through the sheer white curtains. She decided to go for a run.

As luck would have it, Teddy Fowler was the first person Cassie ran into on the Coastal Walk. She ignored him and started jogging toward the Castle Beach Resort. Teddy called after her a couple of times before giving up.

Cassie reached the end of the trail and sat on a bench overlooking the bay, biding time. She hoped Teddy would be gone by the time she went back. She had no such luck. Teddy was doing situps against a bench. He hailed her immediately.

"Wait up, Cassie. We need to talk."

"I did all the talking I wanted to yesterday," Cassie quipped. "I have nothing to say to you, Teddy Fowler."

"But I do. I have news for you."

Cassie's eyes filled with fear.

"Are you taking me in again?"

"No, Cassie. Calm down, okay? There's been a new development in the case."

Cassie collapsed on the bench and took deep breaths, trying to calm down her racing heart.

"You know that van we saw on the security video?"

"The one that belonged to Tim Buckner?" Cassie asked. "Wasn't it supposed to be stolen?"

"That's what he claimed, yes. And he may have been telling the truth."

Did that mean Tim Buckner was innocent? Cassie didn't understand how it was good for her.

"Buckner told us where he had parked the car. We have been trying to find someone who might have been in that area on the night in question."

"Go on," Cassie prompted impatiently.

"A witness came forward. To make a long story short, we

found the man who was seen stealing that car. He was a valet at the Castle Beach Resort."

"What?" Cassie's mouth hung open.

"That's all I can tell you now. We'll be questioning him later today."

"Is this good for me?"

"Keep your fingers crossed, Cassie," Teddy nodded. "You might be off the hook by the end of the day."

Chapter 27

Anna sat on a bench in her garden, admiring the roses in bloom. Her mug of steaming coffee cooled in her hands. There was a slight mist in the air and the sun was just beginning to peep through the clouds, a few watery rays of sunlight filtering through.

Anna was happy. Cassie had gone for a run and Meg was still asleep. Having Meg in the house felt like a dream. Anna hummed a tune and went inside, eager to cook a hearty breakfast.

Meg was the first to come in to the kitchen.

"Something smells nice, Anna."

"I hope you're hungry," Anna said. "I'm making chocolate chip pancakes with bacon. And there's avocado toast." She remembered Meg liked avocadoes.

"Did someone say pancakes?" Cassie asked, bursting in.

Anna was surprised to see her grinning broadly.

"Oh Mom! You'll never guess what has happened."

She told them about her little chat with Teddy Fowler.

"At least we have some breathing room," Anna said. "But we can't rest easy. We need to get back to our search as soon as we finish eating."

"Don't worry, Anna," Meg assured her. "We'll find something today."

They ate the yummy food, Meg complimenting Anna on the pancakes.

"These are intense," she said. "And unlike any I tasted before."

"I have a secret ingredient," Anna beamed. "And I use special chocolate chips, of course."

Meg helped Anna clear the table and loaded the dishwasher.

"I can go ahead and open the store," she told Anna. "I have my laptop with me so I can start some research right away."

"I'll be there soon," Anna promised her and said goodbye. "Do you need a ride?"

Meg assured her she could walk the short distance and said goodbye.

Anna went back in to check on Cassie. Cassie was reading something off her phone.

"Bobby says I should swim ten extra laps to work off the pancakes."

"Are you interested in what's going on, Cassie?" Anna asked, exasperated.

"Of course I am, Mom. I really appreciate what you are doing. Both of you."

"Looks like you're planning to stay home."

"I'm waiting for a call from my agent," Cassie replied. "I'm going to wait at home for a while and then come to the store. We can have lunch together."

"Let me know if Teddy calls you with an update," Anna warned. "This is no laughing matter, Cassie. Get your head out of the clouds."

Cassie's face fell.

"Of course I know that, Mom. I'm trying to deal with it the best way I can. You tackle your problems head-on. I try to pretend they aren't there. We are two different people."

"I don't have time to get into this now, Cassie."

Anna showered hurriedly and got ready.

"Keep your phone close," she warned Cassie on the way out.

"Where's your scarf, Mom?" Cassie asked. "It's going to be hot later."

Anna muttered something under her breath and wound a scarf around her face and neck. She couldn't wait for the day when she had to stop covering herself up.

At Bayside Books, Meg sat at the reading table, feverishly tapping keys on her laptop. She looked up when Anna went in.

"I started on this right away, Anna. I haven't dusted the shelves yet."

"Don't worry about it, sweetie," Anna smiled. "What you are doing is more important. And you do it better than me. I can take care of the chores around here today."

Anna went into the pantry and started a pot of coffee. She picked up a duster and began cleaning the bookshelves. The aroma of freshly brewed coffee soon filled the air. She fixed Meg's coffee with lots of cream and four sugars, then filled her own cup.

"Any luck so far?" she asked Meg, placing her coffee before her.

"Thanks Anna," Meg said brightly. "It's all really confusing. There are so many people. I can't keep this straight in my head. Maybe the coffee will help."

"Are you going through the seven people we talked about last night?"

"Yes," Meg nodded. "I'm just on the fifth one. And this is only the first time I'm reading this. I can't keep it straight in my head."

"What's confusing me is there are two victims," Anna thought out loud. "There is the person or persons who died first. Then there is the person who was accused for that crime and died later."

"The accused person is of interest to us," Meg said. "Does

it matter what this person was accused for?"

"We don't know at this point," Anna said. "We don't even know how these accused dead people are connected to William Parker."

"So we can't ignore anything yet," Meg summed up.

The bells on the door jingled and Julie swept in. She raised her hands in the air and let out a little whoop.

"It's done, Anna. My draft is on its way to the editor. Get ready to par-tay."

She sobered when she noticed Anna's grim expression.

"Where's Cassie, Anna?"

"Cassie's at home," Anna sighed. "Meg and I are following a hunch."

She explained what they were doing. Julie pulled out her tablet from her voluminous bag and settled down next to Meg.

"Let's divide these names up, kiddo. We'll get through them quicker."

She started reading up on the old news stories, exhibiting the same horror and sadness the Butler women had experienced the night before.

"Some of these stories seem unreal," she cried. "Look at this one. This man, a construction worker, was accused of messing with a ladder."

"What's that?" Anna asked curiously. "We haven't seen that before."

"I started backwards," Julie explained. "That way, Meg can continue with her list and we can meet half way."

"What about the ladder?"

"Sounds like nonsense to me," Julie grunted. "Some man fell off a ladder and broke his neck. This other guy was accused of negligence or something. It says it was his responsibility to make sure the ladder wouldn't give way."

"Isn't that farfetched?" Meg asked.

"Looks like the court agreed with you," Julie said, reading the rest of the story. "And the man who fell was overweight. He didn't check how much weight the ladder could bear."

"So this accused man was let go?" Anna asked. "I'm guessing he died later?"

"He died in a construction accident," Julie cried. "The family thought it was suspicious but the police closed the case."

"This is all too demoralizing," Anna grumbled. "Can you believe we have been reading about one sordid tale after another since last night?"

"Look … this is all so sad. The man had a family, wife and two little kids. The child was some kind of prodigy, it seems. There's a picture. Oh Anna, this is so heartbreaking."

Anna and Meg leaned over and started watching the screen. Julie clicked on a picture of a perfect family, shot on some beach. A small boy in swimming trunks held his mother's hand. A young girl stood next to him, beaming at the camera. The man had his hands on her shoulders.

Julie shivered suddenly.

"I just had a déjà vu moment. There's something familiar about this photo, Anna."

"Really?" Anna moved closer and asked Julie to enlarge the picture. "It's that little girl. I think I have seen her somewhere."

"Let me look," Meg said, taking the tablet from Julie's hands.

She stared at the screen for a moment and made a weird noise.

"Unbelievable! This looks like Ashley."

"Who's Ashley?" Julie asked.

"That blues singer at the Castle Beach Resort?" Anna asked. "She's almost your age, isn't she, Meg?"

"She's 19 now, I think. But this photo is old." She turned toward Julie. "When was this taken?"

"It doesn't say that," Julie said. "But this news item is almost seven years old."

"Ashley's father died when she was 12," Meg cried. "She

told me when we met for our surfing lesson."

"What else did she tell you?" Anna asked urgently. "Did she say how he died?"

Meg shook her head.

"Her name is Ashley Morton. She's from Monterey. All she said was he died suddenly and their life kind of fell apart after that. She started singing at a very young age. She had to, in order to support her family."

Julie was tapping the screen, nodding her head.

"It all adds up. This accused man is Peter Morton from Monterey, California."

The three women stared at each other.

"Does this mean Ashley is involved in all this?" Meg asked.

"It's a connection worth exploring," Julie said. "And we don't have any other leads."

"I'm calling Gino," Anna said, springing into action. "He can take it from here."

Chapter 28

Anna sat in the China Garden restaurant with Julie and Meg. She had asked Cassie to join them for lunch. They were waiting for her to arrive before they could order.

"This girl has no sense of time," Anna muttered.

"She'll be here soon, Anna." Julie defended Cassie. "Why don't you go ahead and check out the menu, see what you want."

"I know what I want," Anna said. "Orange Chicken."

"I'll get the same," Meg said.

Cassie rushed into the restaurant and weaved her way to their table.

"Sorry it took so long. I was on a call."

"Aren't you always?" Anna rolled her eyes.

They placed their orders immediately and sat back, looking at each other in excitement.

"Did they do it?" Cassie breathed. "Did they arrest that singer?"

"Gino called once to tell us they took her in," Anna told her. "I guess they are still questioning her."

"Why don't we go to the police station?" Cassie asked. "Teddy Fowler owes me an explanation after everything he put me through."

"I'd rather not go there," Anna said.

Julie agreed.

"Let's enjoy our lunch. We can go back to the store after that and wait."

"That sounds boring," Meg said.

"Right?" Cassie jumped in. "I'd rather find out everything right now."

Finally, Anna convinced the girls to settle down. Lunch arrived but they were all too distracted to focus on the food. No one wanted dessert. They walked back to the store after that. Anna decided to do the accounts. Julie and Meg picked up a book to read and Cassie paced around the store, messaging Bobby on her phone.

"Why don't you call Gino, Mom?" Cassie suggested a couple of hours later.

"His phone is switched off."

It was past five when Gino walked into the door. They attacked him with a barrage of questions. He held up his hand and told them to calm down.

"Anna, can I bother you for some coffee, please?" he asked. "It looks like I'm going to need a lot of energy to face you ladies."

There was a twinkle in his eye and Anna nodded, going into the pantry to start a fresh pot.

"Ashley Morton confessed to killing William Parker." Gino cut to the chase after he had taken a few sips of the steaming coffee Anna handed him.

Everyone started speaking at once.

"Do you think she really did it?" Anna asked Gino.

"It seemed a bit farfetched, looking at her. You need to hear the whole story."

Gino started at the beginning.

"Ashley was 12 when her father died. They were a middle class family, very close knit based on what she said. Peter Morton doted on his wife and kids and worked hard to give them what they needed."

"She talked about them when we first met," Meg nodded.

"Ashley was something of a child prodigy. They arranged music lessons for her."

"She dreamed of going to Juilliard," Meg interrupted again. "Her father was all for it."

"How do you know so much?" Cassie asked.

"We took a surfing lesson together, remember? She was quite talkative."

"Why don't we let Gino speak?" Julie interrupted.

"Peter's death was a shock," Gino continued. "Something happened at his construction site. His wife thought there was some foul play. The police did some cursory investigation and ruled it out."

"What about the time he was arrested for negligence?" Anna asked.

"Oh yeah." Gino yawned. "That's when their troubles started. Peter had to go through that trial. He was acquitted and the family slowly got back to normal. Peter died a few months after that."

"It was really tough on Ashley," Meg supplied. "They could barely make ends meet. She started singing professionally to support her family."

"That's true, Meg," Gino agreed. "Ashley had to grow up overnight. One minute she was this innocent 12 year old, the next she was shouldering the responsibility of her mom and brother."

"So she's been doing concerts for the past six-seven years?" Anna asked.

"Ashley went from strength to strength to be the famous singer she is now," Gino explained. "But she never forgot the circumstances around her father's death. She even tried to get the police to reopen the case a few times."

Anna took a sip of her own coffee and asked the question that was on all their minds.

"Where does William Parker come in?"

"I'm getting there," Gino smiled. "But we have to talk about Joey Bellinger first."

"The journalist?" Meg asked. "What about him?"

"He was working on a story, presumably the same super secret story he would tell us nothing about," Gino replied. "He met the Morton family to talk about Peter."

"What was his interest in Peter Morton?" Julie asked.

Gino looked at Meg.

"Your vigilante theory was spot on. Joey Bellinger noticed how all those people who were acquitted by the courts were dying soon after. What's more, their deaths were highly suspicious. He was meeting the families of all these victims, trying to gather more information."

"Did he tell Ashley about his theory?" Meg asked.

Gino nodded.

"Ashley found it encouraging. Here was someone who finally believed her father might have been killed. Joey didn't tell her much, citing the need for caution."

"What did Ashley do after that?" Cassie asked. "How did she get to William Parker?"

"Ashley was clever," Gino sighed. "She followed Joey Bellinger to Dolphin Bay. When she realized he was sticking around in this area, she got herself a gig at the Castle Beach Resort. For all intents and purposes, she was here to give concerts."

"No one suspected her," Anna observed. "Sounds diabolical, but who could blame the girl?"

Gino looked grave.

"By this time, Ashley was on a mission. She wanted to find out who killed her father, Peter Morton."

"How did she zero in on Parker?" Julie spoke this time. She had a dazed look on her face.

Gino continued his story.

"Ashley kept tabs on Joey Bellinger. When he followed William Parker to that cabin in the woods, she was right behind him. After that, she began keeping an eye on Parker. She went inside the cabin, found the hidden room behind the bookshelves and saw the cork board with all those clippings."

Meg was listening to Gino, wide eyed.

"She must have been shocked to see her own father's picture there."

Gino looked sad as he told them what Ashley had done next.

"She connected the dots based on what she knew. That's when she made up her mind to avenge her father."

Cassie spoke up.

"How did she actually do it? And why dump him here, in Mom's bookstore?"

"Ashley thought she had a foolproof plan," Gino said, "but even the best laid plans can go wrong sometimes."

"How did she make sure he would be at the Castle Beach Resort?" Meg asked.

"She sent him some passes for the concert. She had a hunch he wouldn't turn down a freebie and she was right."

"Had she planned to poison him?" Anna asked. "Where did she get that stuff?"

Gino stood up and stretched.

"She got hold of some heavy duty pain pills and crushed them up. She wanted it to look accidental. She figured the pills would knock him out and it would look like he died from an overdose."

"An accidental death, just like her father's," Julie whispered. "Sounds like poetic justice."

"How did she make him drink it?" Anna asked.

"That part is unclear, Anna. I think she mixed it in some drink and just placed the drink before him. He had no reason to suspect her, you know. Here was this young, beautiful celebrity getting him a drink. He wasn't going to turn it down."

"What about the car?" Cassie asked. "And where does that valet they arrested earlier today come in?"

"Ashley bribed that poor valet," Gino explained. "Told him to get a car for her. I don't think she imagined he would steal one."

"So she somehow talked William Parker into going out to that car with her," Anna mused, trying to figure it all out. "Where did she plan to take him?"

"I think she was just going to let him loose near the cliffs and hope he walked off them," Gino shrugged. "But Ashley hit a snag."

Anna, Cassie, Meg and Julie were all agog, eager to hear what Gino told them next.

"The drugs didn't work as expected. William Parker started stirring. Ashley was driving by when she saw the door to the bookstore wide open. There wasn't anyone around so she took a chance."

"It was a very big chance," Julie cried. "What if Anna had been in here doing something? Would she have hurt her too?"

"I think Ashley wasn't thinking rationally by that time." Gino gave a shrug. "Or she wanted to finish what she had started."

"She brought him into the store by herself?" Cassie quizzed.

"Ashley is quite strong," Meg spoke up. "It must be from all that kayaking she does."

Gino wrapped up the rest of the story.

"So they came in somehow. Ashley realized the drugs

weren't working as fast as she wanted. She panicked. She hit him on the head and knocked him out. Once she was sure he wasn't breathing, she beat it out of the store."

"What about the weapon?" Anna asked. "They never found it here."

"Ashley chucked it out in the ocean," Gino said. "She never said what it was, though."

There was a stunned silence as they processed the whole sordid tale.

"One thing is not clear," Anna ventured. "Was William Parker guilty of killing Peter Morton?"

"He was," Gino said seriously. "And Parker wasn't his only victim."

Anna looked stricken.

"Do we even want to know what that means?"

"Probably not," Gino said, looking uncertainly at Meg. "I've seen some bad things while I was on the police force, Anna, but this beats everything."

"Don't worry about me," Meg assured them. "I think we have already guessed some of it."

"The police called Joey Bellinger in," Gino told them. "In the light of Ashley's confession, he told us about the story he has been working on."

"William Parker was a vigilante who went around killing

people." Julie said slowly. "Like Meg said, we figured it out."

Gino closed his eyes for a minute and exhaled through his mouth.

"He wasn't the only one."

They all stared at Gino, their mouths hanging open.

"This was Joey's theory. There is a group of these vigilantes scattered around the country. They follow murder trials and pay close attention to people that are acquitted by the courts. If they think the person is guilty, they deliver their own brand of justice."

"Which is what?" Anna grimaced.

Everyone knew the answer to that.

"They are quite organized, according to Bellinger," Gino continued. "Everyone has an area assigned to them. William Parker was responsible for these parts, for example."

"Do they know each other?" Julie asked. "They must get together somewhere."

"I don't know," Gino said honestly. "They meet in an online chat room. They have some kind of code they use to communicate. At least, that's all Joey Bellinger has figured out until now. The federal authorities will take over this investigation now, of course."

"That's what it was!" Meg exclaimed suddenly. "Remember

William Parker's computer? All those chess games he played and the cryptic messages?"

"That must be how they communicate," Gino said, springing to his feet. "I forgot about that computer, Meg. Let me make a quick call."

He pulled out his phone and dialed the police station. He walked a few steps away from them and began explaining what Meg had found at the cabin to someone on the other end.

"What about Anna's accident?" Meg asked Gino. "I could be sure a guy was driving that car."

"It was the valet again," Gino explained. "Ashley told him to scare Anna. He wasn't supposed to hurt her."

"Why did he do all this?" Julie asked. "For money?"

"Partly," Gino shrugged. "I think he was smitten by Ashley and would have done anything to please her. Within reason, we hope."

"What a day!" Cassie exclaimed. "I want to sleep for two days straight."

"You know what this means, Anna?" Julie asked, pulling her into a hug. "You are free. And so is Cassie."

Anna thought of Ashley, the young, talented girl who had sacrificed her future to avenge the past. How would the world judge her?

Epilogue

Anna looked around the gaily decorated café and beamed with pride. The much awaited day had arrived. It was the grand opening of her café. Her long cherished dream was finally coming true.

A flicker of doubt crept in her eyes.

"What is it, Mom?" Cassie asked.

"Do you think they will come?"

Julie took over before Cassie could respond.

"Come? This café is going to be bursting at the seams in less than an hour. That's why we put those plastic chairs out on the sidewalk."

"The Rose Show made a big difference," Mary said softly.

Anna had triumphed at the Rose Show. Agnes had been quite vocal against allowing Anna to enter the Eloise rose in the contest. But Mary had prevailed over the members of the Garden Club. Anna had been allowed to enter the rose her beloved John had spent years creating. Agnes had been silenced when it even won a prize. Anna had been in seventh heaven.

Mary had told them how the Rose Show Committee was looking for people to donate snacks for the show. At Julie's suggestion, Anna had taken the opportunity and provided her orange thyme cupcakes. They had been a big hit. Now the whole town wanted to taste Anna Butler's cupcakes.

Anna had dressed for the occasion. Cassie, Meg and the Firecrackers had all insisted. She was wearing a pretty floral frock that was perfect for summer. And she wore bright pink shoes. Cassie told her they were the latest fashion. The other girls got into the spirit of things and dressed in a similar fashion.

Meg had finally rinsed off the blue color from her hair. It was a slightly darker shade of gold than Cassie's. Anna was proud of how confident and beautiful she looked. She had an innate grace in her bearing, just like Cassie. Like mother, like daughter, Anna thought with a smile.

Anna's face lit up when the first guest walked in through the door.

"Gino!" she welcomed. "You are early."

Gino handed her a large bunch of daisies and congratulated her.

"So the big day is here, Anna. Are you ready for it?"

A bunch of people came in before she could thank him. Julie stepped forward to welcome them and show them around. Anna had given an open invite to the whole town and placed an ad in the Chronicle. Some of the faces were not familiar so she gathered some tourists had filtered in too.

The orange thyme cupcakes were the star of the day. Meg

brought out tray after tray of the delicious treats and brewed countless pots of coffee.

Dylan Woods came in and congratulated Anna. He said something to Cassie, making her bristle. Charlie Robinson arrived with an orchid plant and made a beeline for Anna.

"The chef at the resort can't stop talking about your cupcakes," he confided in her. "We need to talk about putting them on the resort's menu."

"Do you believe it now?" Julie asked Anna a couple of hours later.

The café was packed and the crowd showed no signs of leaving. Anna was feeling a bit overwhelmed.

Mary came to stand next to Anna. The Firecrackers looked at her questioningly.

"Are you going to do it?" Julie asked.

"I still think you should consult Cassie," Mary sighed. "This affects her too, you know."

Anna had made a big decision. She was going to introduce Meg to everyone, tell them she was her granddaughter. Anna felt she owed it to Meg. Cassie might throw a hissy fit but she would have to come around.

She looked around the room, trying to spot the two of them. She wanted both of them by her side when she made the announcement.

Cassie was talking to Meg.

"Why don't you take a break? You've been at it all evening."

Meg brought out a fresh tray of cupcakes and pulled her apron off. She was ready to get some fresh air. She followed Cassie through the arch leading into the bookstore and out through the door. They stood under the magnolia tree, letting the breeze fan their faces.

"This feels good." Meg closed her eyes and lifted her face, breathing in the scent of the pink and white blossoms towering over her.

"You said you were traveling," Cassie said urgently. "When I met you first, you told me you were on a trip of the California coast."

"I did say that." Meg nodded, looking at Cassie questioningly.

"When are you leaving, Meg?"

      ***

Thank you for reading this book. If you enjoyed this book, please consider leaving a brief review. Even a few words or a line or two will do.

As an indie author, I rely on reviews to spread the word about my book. Your assistance will be very helpful and greatly appreciated.

I would also really appreciate it if you tell your friends and family about the book. Word of mouth is an author's best friend, and it will be of immense help to me.

Many Thanks!

Author Leena Clover

Other books by Leena Clover

Pelican Cove Cozy Mystery Series

Strawberries and Strangers

Cupcakes and Celebrities

Berries and Birthdays

Sprinkles and Skeletons

Waffles and Weekends

Muffins and Mobsters

Parfaits and Paramours

Truffles and Troubadours

Sundaes and Sinners

Meera Patel Cozy Mystery Series

Gone with the Wings

A Pocket Full of Pie

For a Few Dumplings More

Back to the Fajitas

Christmas with the Franks

Dolphin Bay Cozy Mystery Series

Raspberry Chocolate Murder

Acknowledgements

I would like to extend my heartfelt thanks to each and every person who made this book possible. My family has my eternal gratitude for their constant support and encouragement. I owe thanks to all beta readers and reviewers for spending their valuable time reading early copies of my books and providing valuable feedback. Last but not the least, my wonderful readers who give this indie author a chance every time they pick up one of my books. Thanks for the motivation and all the kind messages. You make my day and help me write more books.

Join my Newsletter

Get access to exclusive bonus content, sneak peeks, giveaways and much more. Also get a chance to join my exclusive ARC group, the people who get first dibs on all my new books.

Sign up at the following link and join the fun.

Click here →
http://www.subscribepage.com/leenaclovernl

I love to hear from my readers, so please feel free to connect with me at any of the following places.

Website – http://leenaclover.com

Twitter – https://twitter.com/leenaclover

Facebook –
http://facebook.com/leenaclovercozymysterybooks

Email – leenaclover@gmail.com

Made in the USA
Las Vegas, NV
02 May 2024

89413392R00142